THE GREAT PET ESCAPE

Victoria Jamieson

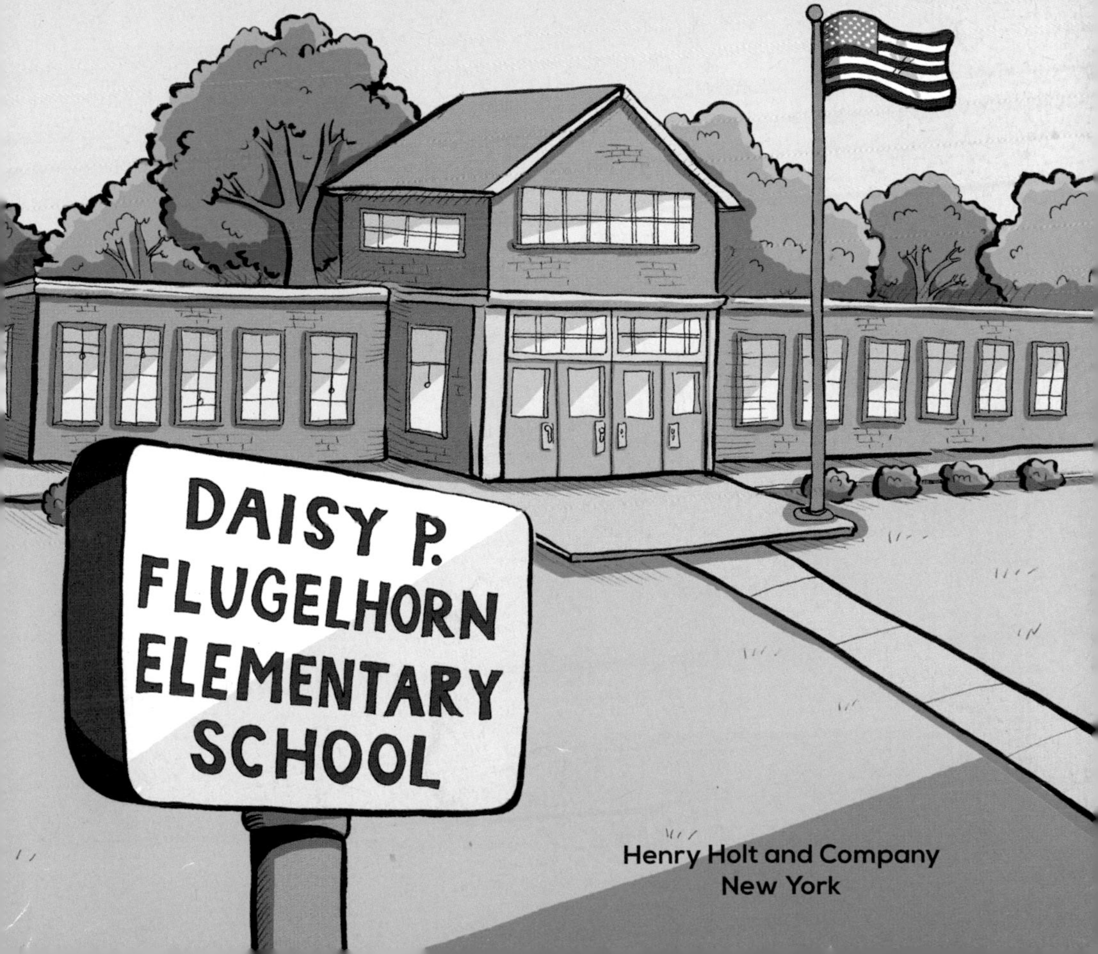
DAISY P.
FLUGELHORN
ELEMENTARY
SCHOOL

Henry Holt and Company
New York

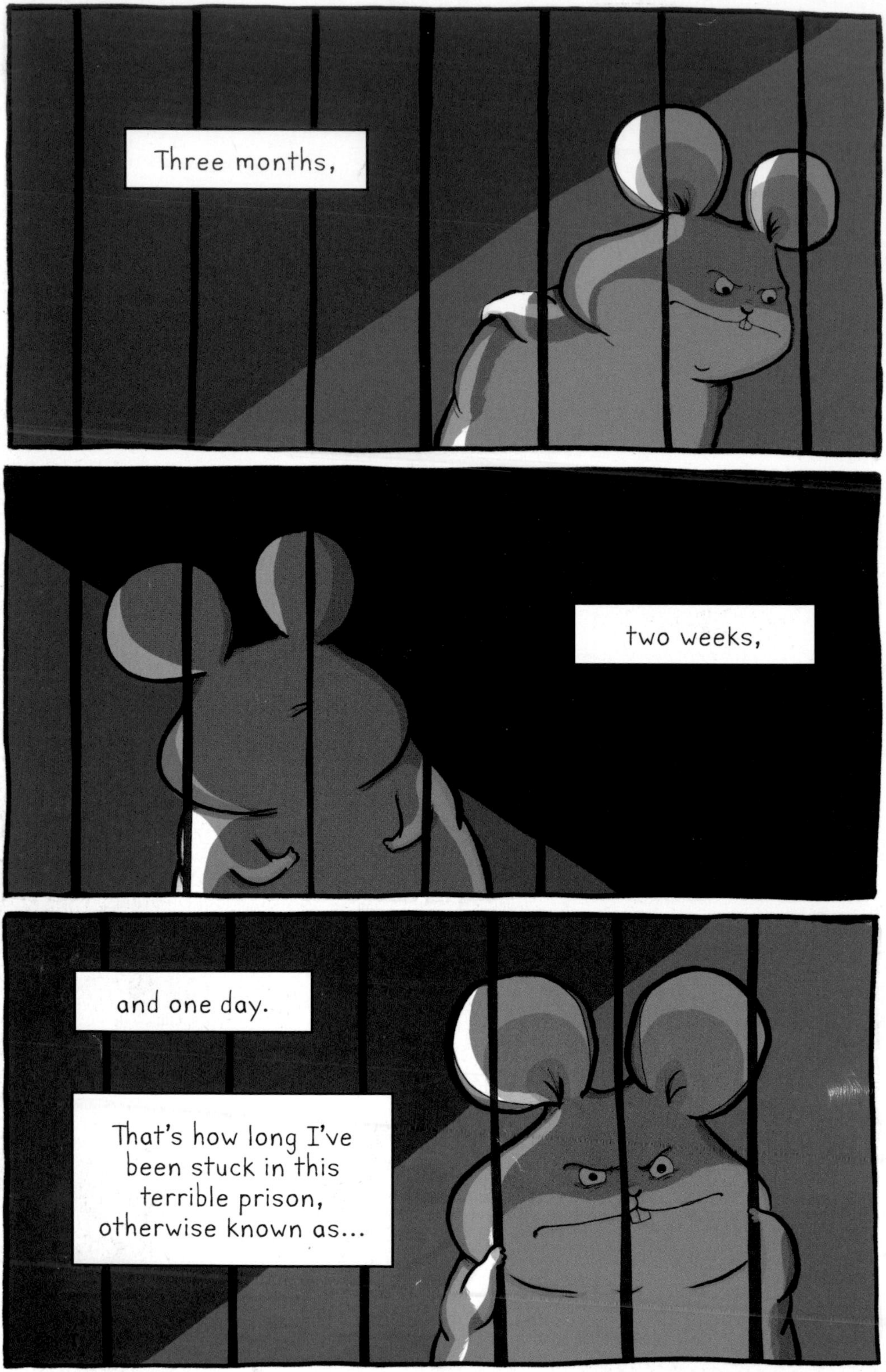
Three months,
two weeks,
and one day.
That's how long I've been stuck in this terrible prison, otherwise known as...

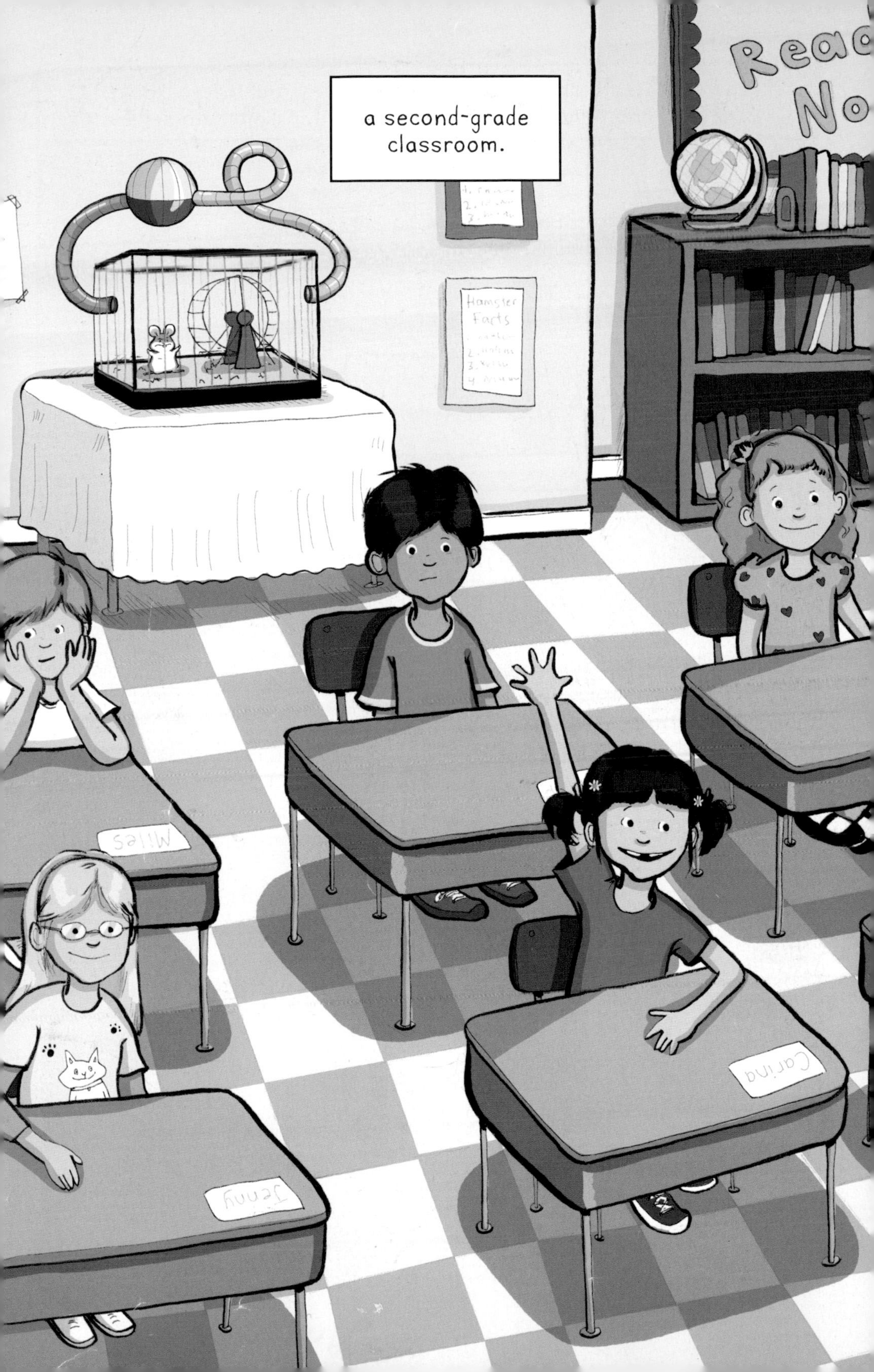

a second-grade classroom.
Hamster Facts
Miles
Carina
Jenny

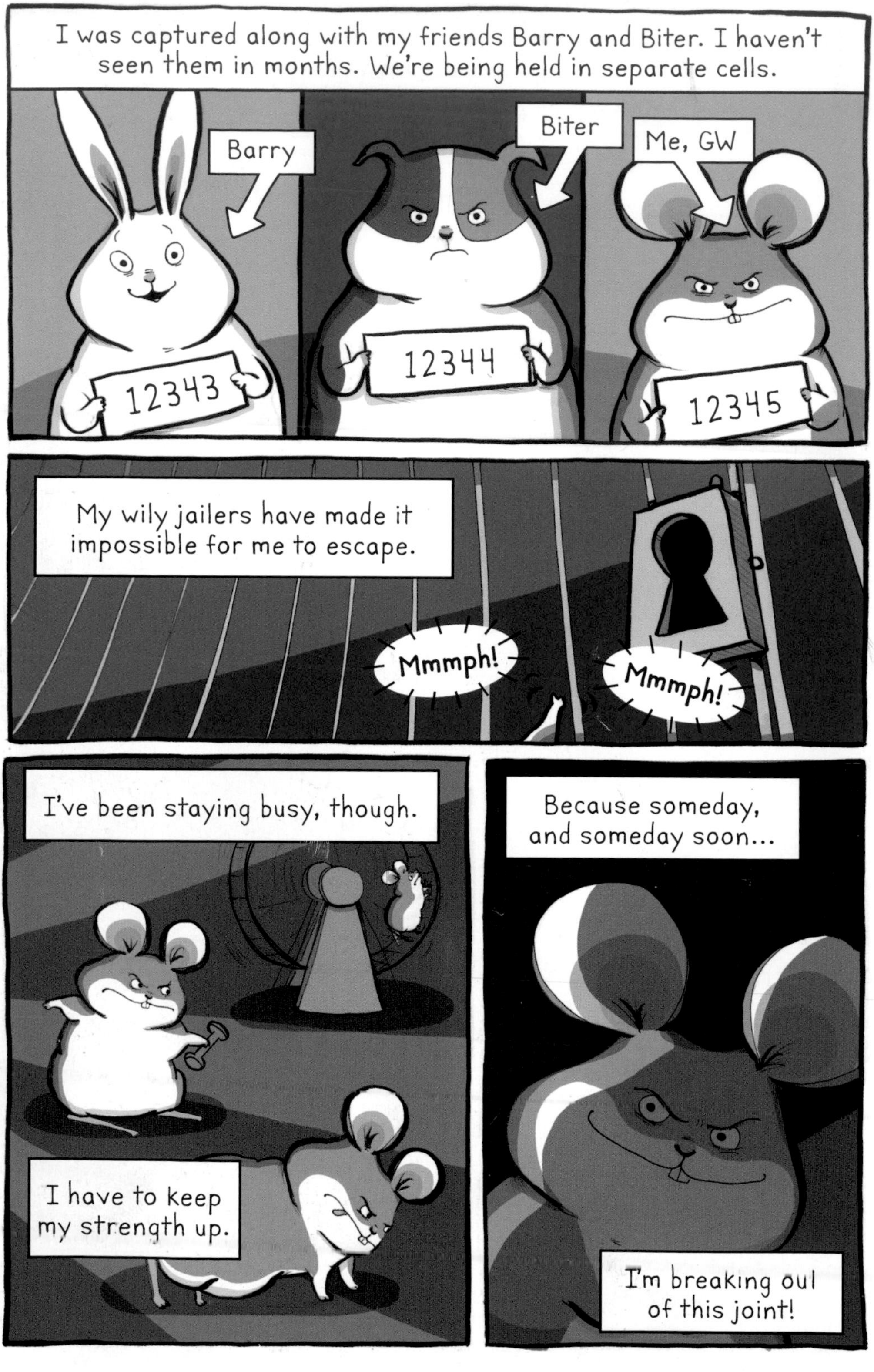
I was captured along with my friends Barry and Biter. I haven't seen them in months. We're being held in separate cells.
Barry
12343
Biter
12344
Me, GW
12345
My wily jailers have made it impossible for me to escape.
Mmmph!
Mmmph!
I've been staying busy, though.
I have to keep my strength up.
Because someday, and someday soon...
I'm breaking out of this joint!

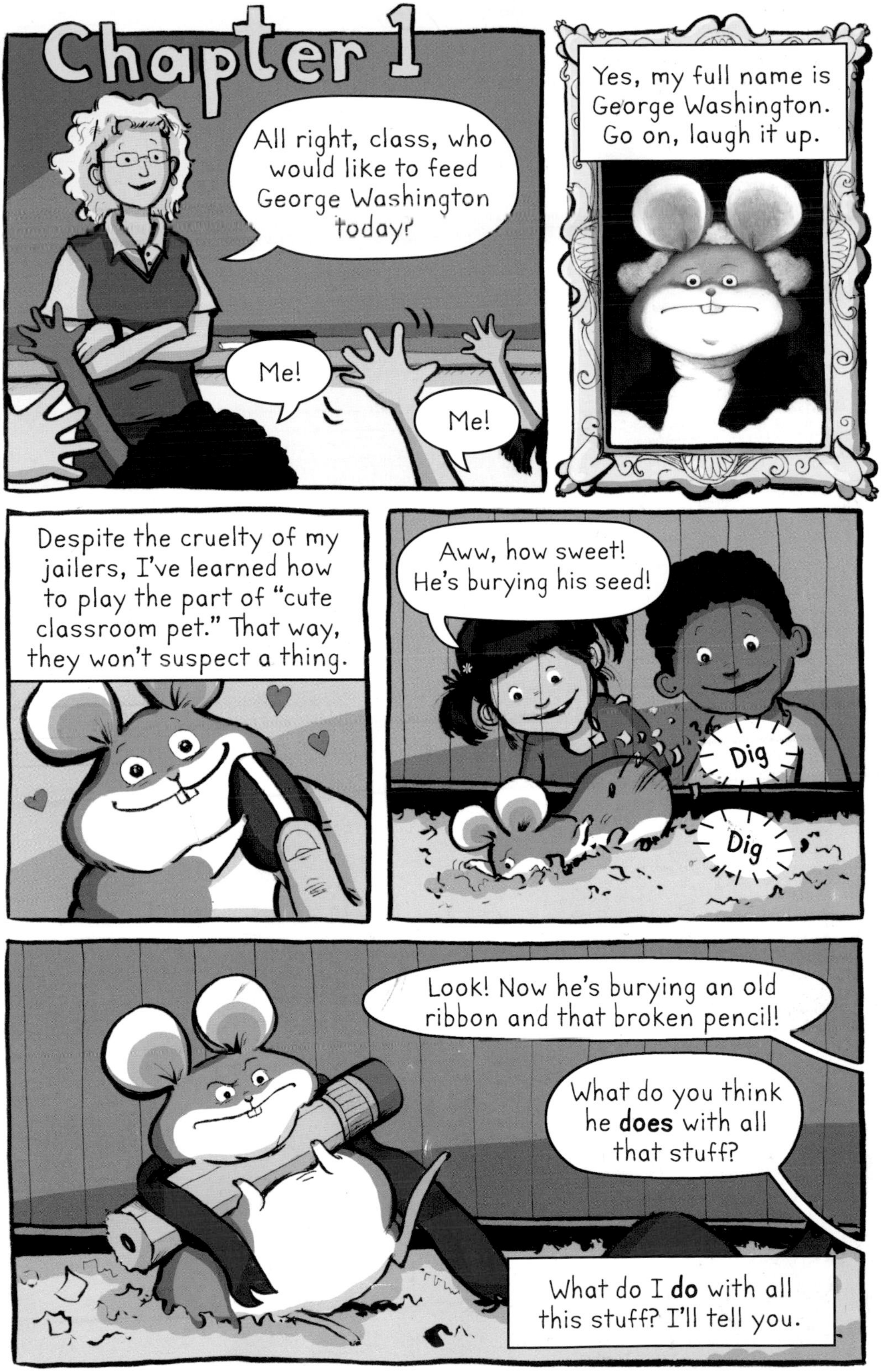
Chapter 1
All right, class, who would like to feed George Washington today?
Me!
Me!
Yes, my full name is George Washington. Go on, laugh it up.
Despite the cruelty of my jailers, I've learned how to play the part of "cute classroom pet." That way, they won't suspect a thing.
Aww, how sweet! He's burying his seed!
Dig
Dig
Look! Now he's burying an old ribbon and that broken pencil!
What do you think he **does** with all that stuff?
What do I **do** with all this stuff? I'll tell you.

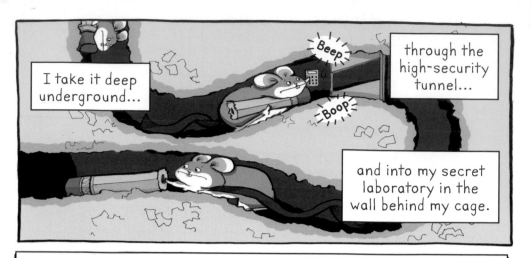

I take it deep underground...

Beep

Boop

through the high-security tunnel...

and into my secret laboratory in the wall behind my cage.

Before I was locked up, I was the greatest inventor this side of Dallas.

Name: GW (aka George Washington)
Species: Hamster
Crimes: Inventor of the Sunflower Seed Slingshot and the Rodent Catapult Transportation Device

But prison can't stop me. I am now building my greatest invention ever...

the **Hairy Houdini Escape-O-Matic.***
I just have to locate the **final missing piece**—and I'll be free!

*patent pending

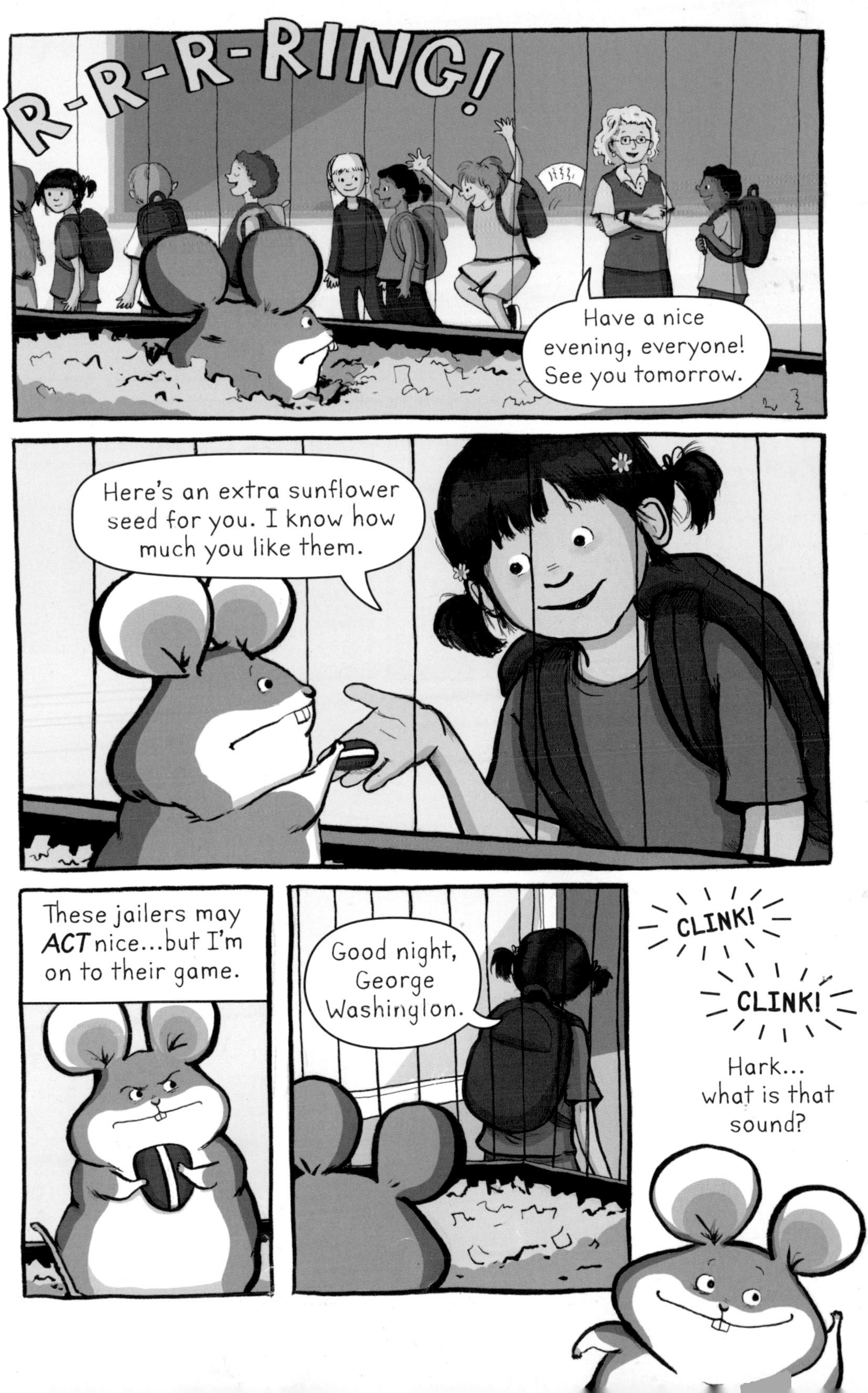
R-R-R-RING!
Have a nice evening, everyone! See you tomorrow.
Here's an extra sunflower seed for you. I know how much you like them.
These jailers may ACT nice...but I'm on to their game.
Good night, George Washington.
CLINK!
CLINK!
Hark... what is that sound?

Could it be? The final missing piece for the **Escape-O-Matic**?

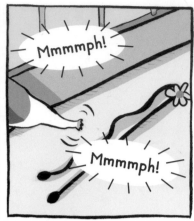

Mmmmph!

Mmmmph!

Gotcha!

Quick!

To the laboratory!

At last! My Hairy Houdini Escape-O-Matic is finished! I am the greatest genius the world has ever seen!

Now...how do I get it upstairs?

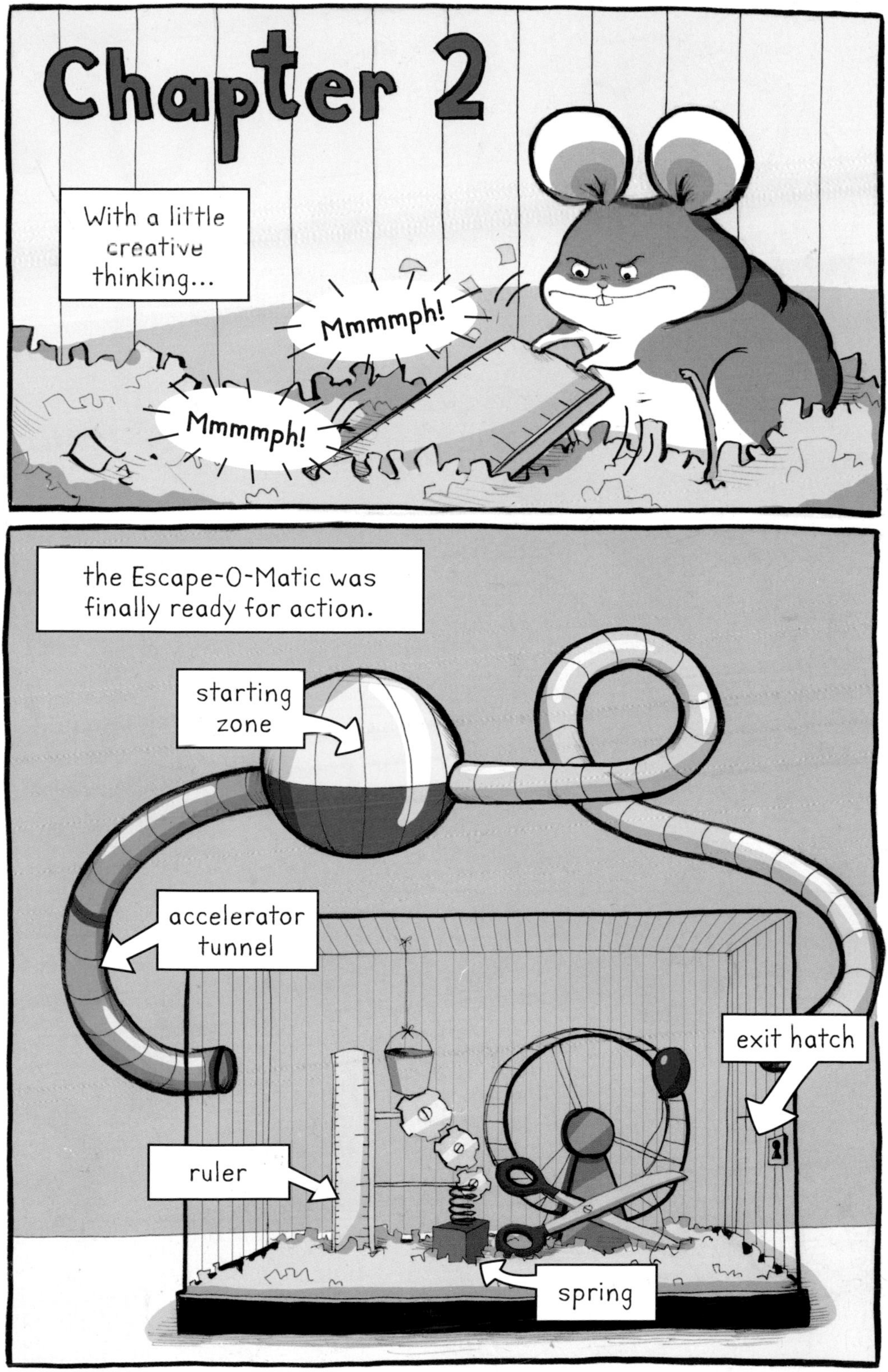
Chapter 2
With a little creative thinking...
Mmmmph!
Mmmmph!
the Escape-O-Matic was finally ready for action.
starting zone
accelerator tunnel
exit hatch
ruler
spring

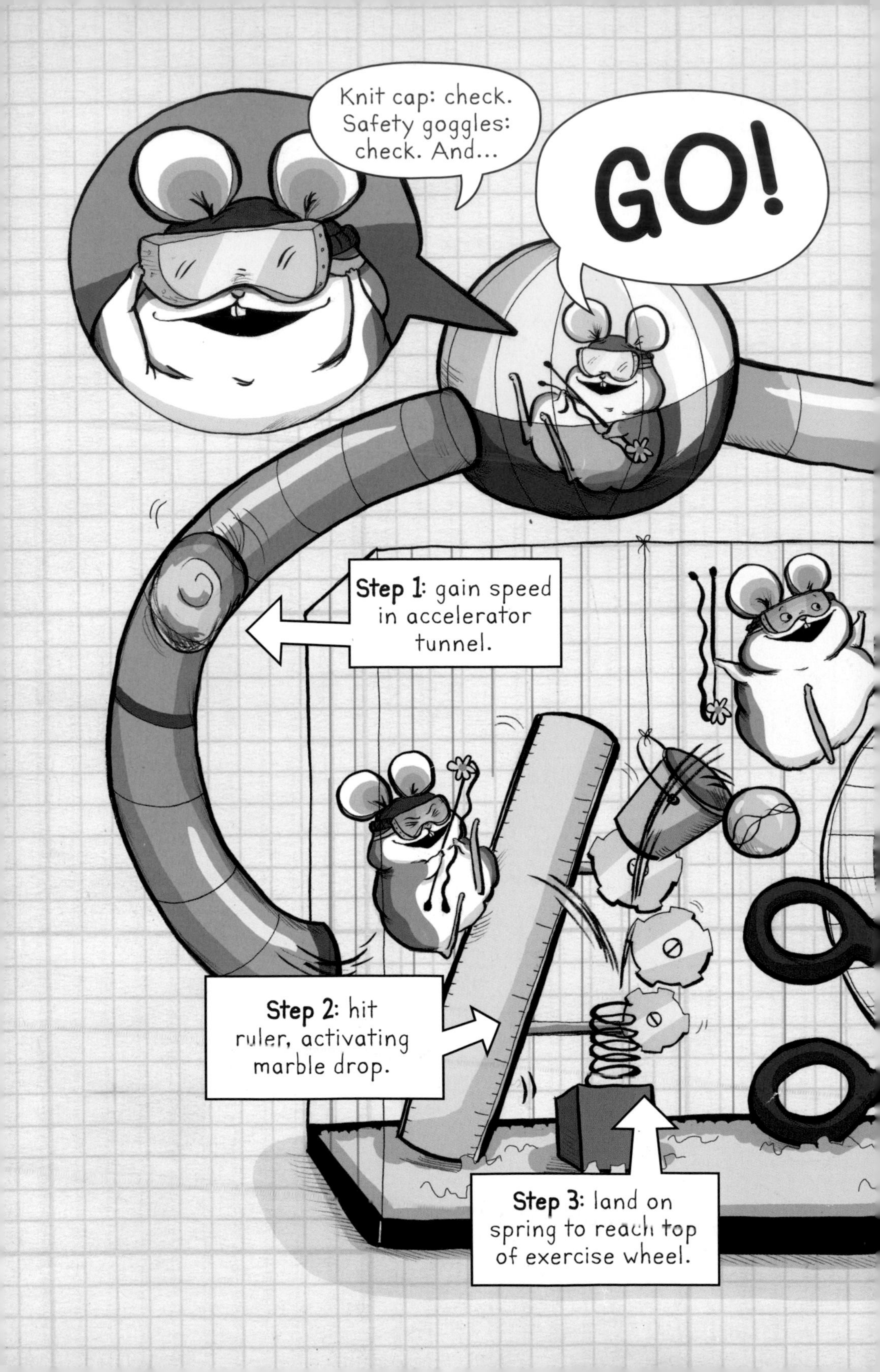
Knit cap: check. Safety goggles: check. And...
GO!
Step 1: gain speed in accelerator tunnel.
Step 2: hit ruler, activating marble drop.
Step 3: land on spring to reach top of exercise wheel.

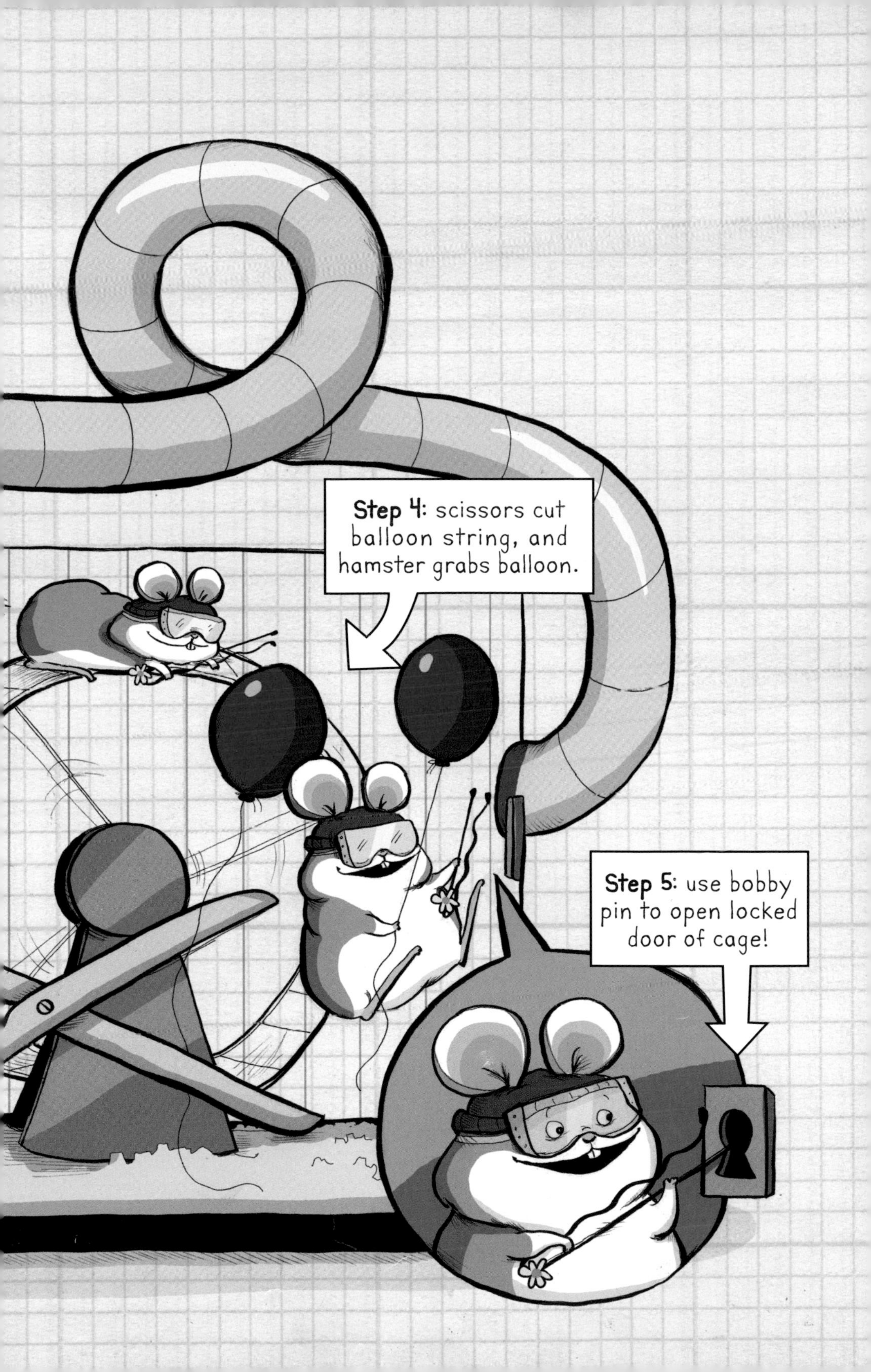
Step 4: scissors cut balloon string, and hamster grabs balloon.
Step 5: use bobby pin to open locked door of cage!

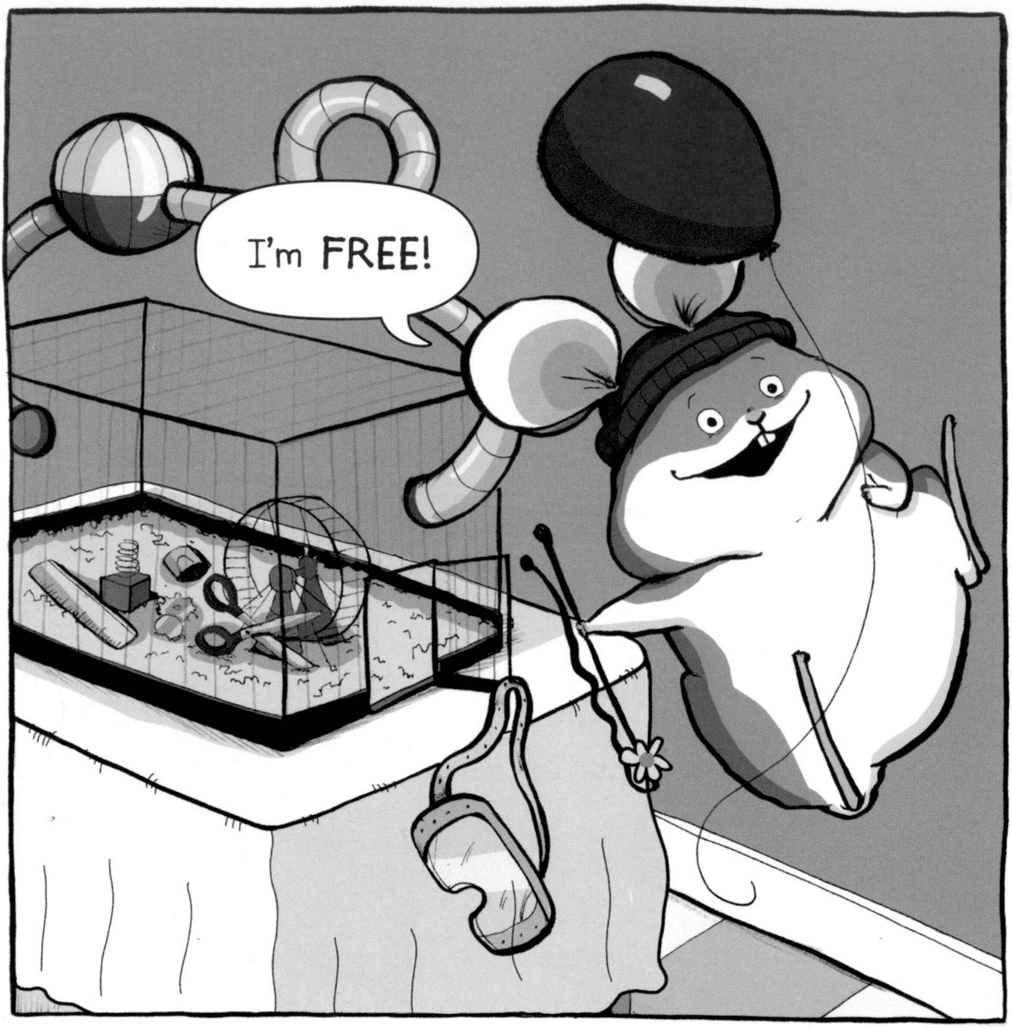
I'm **FREE!**

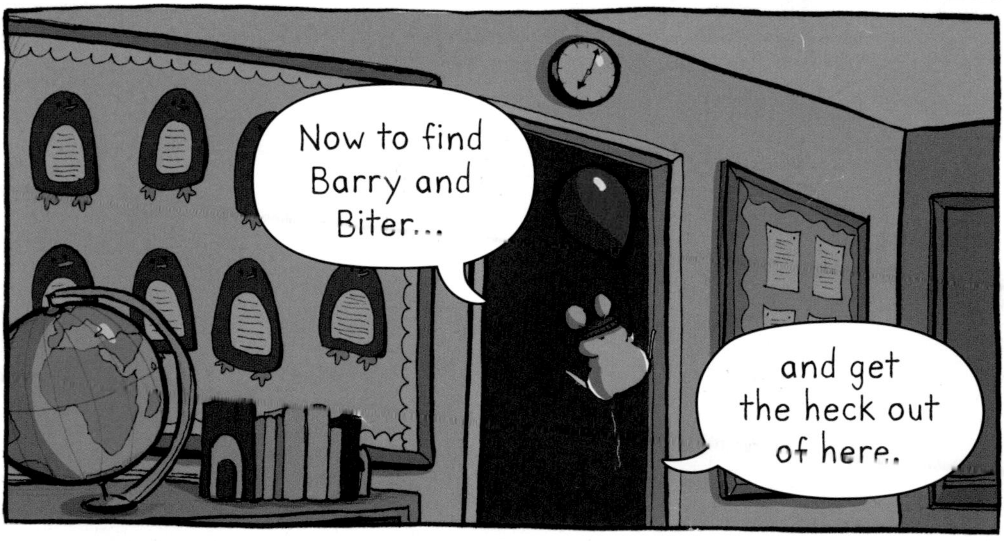
Now to find Barry and Biter...
and get the heck out of here.

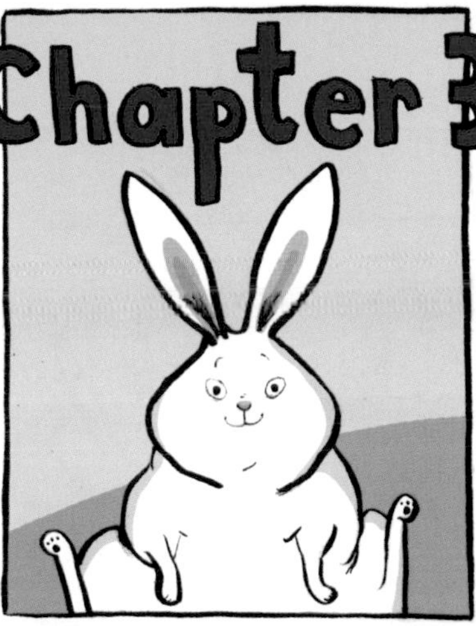
Chapter 3

Barry and I go way back. We've done a lot of time together. He's got a rap sheet as long as his ears.

Name: Barry
Species: Bunny
Crimes: Bunny, sunny, funny, punny . . . Oh, *crimes?* Good heavens! I thought you said *rhymes*.

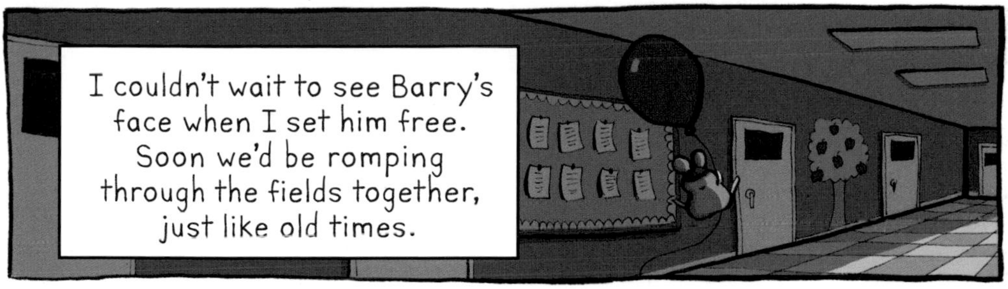
I couldn't wait to see Barry's face when I set him free. Soon we'd be romping through the fields together, just like old times.

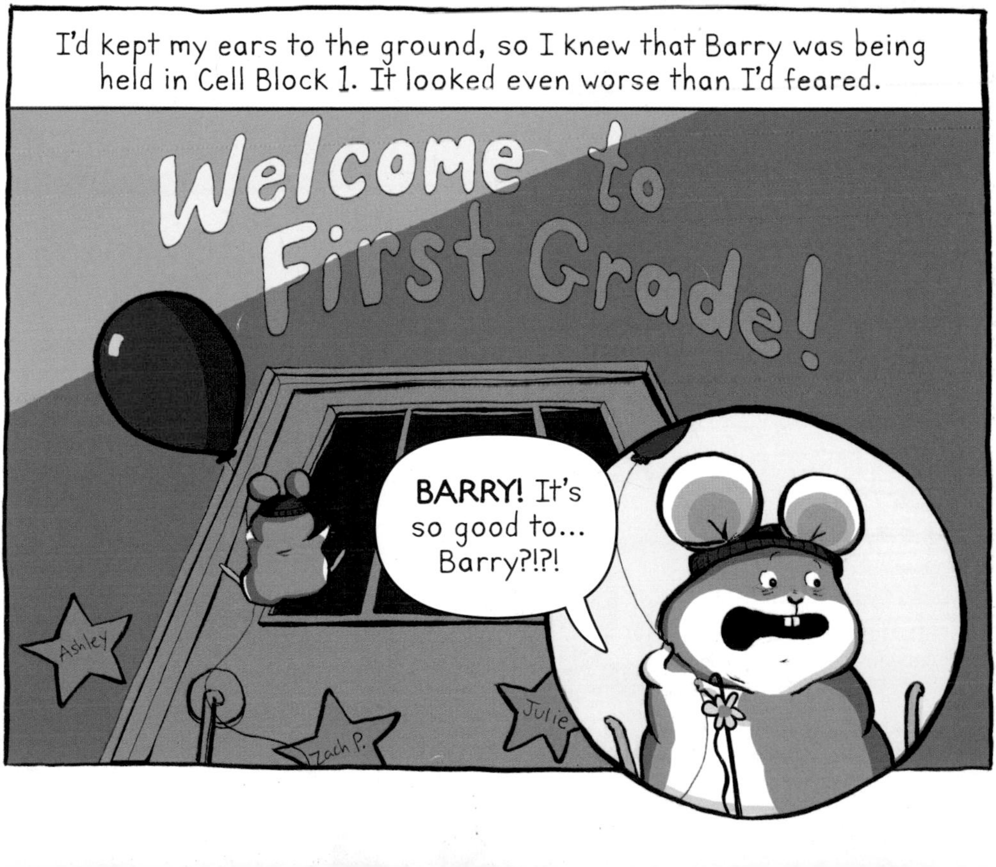
I'd kept my ears to the ground, so I knew that Barry was being held in Cell Block 1. It looked even worse than I'd feared.
Welcome to First Grade!
Ashley
Zach P.
Julie
BARRY! It's so good to... Barry?!?!

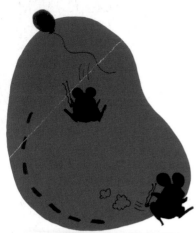

GW! Goodness gracious me, long time no see!

Yeah, that tends to happen when you're in prison. Listen, I've come to set you free!

Hmm? Really? Oh. Okay, sure. Let me just put this bookmark in.

Now I'll tuck in Winken, Blinken, and Todd....

Those are TOYS, Barry. Are you feeling all right?

Barry was acting very weird. Had he gone soft in prison?

Now stand back....

14

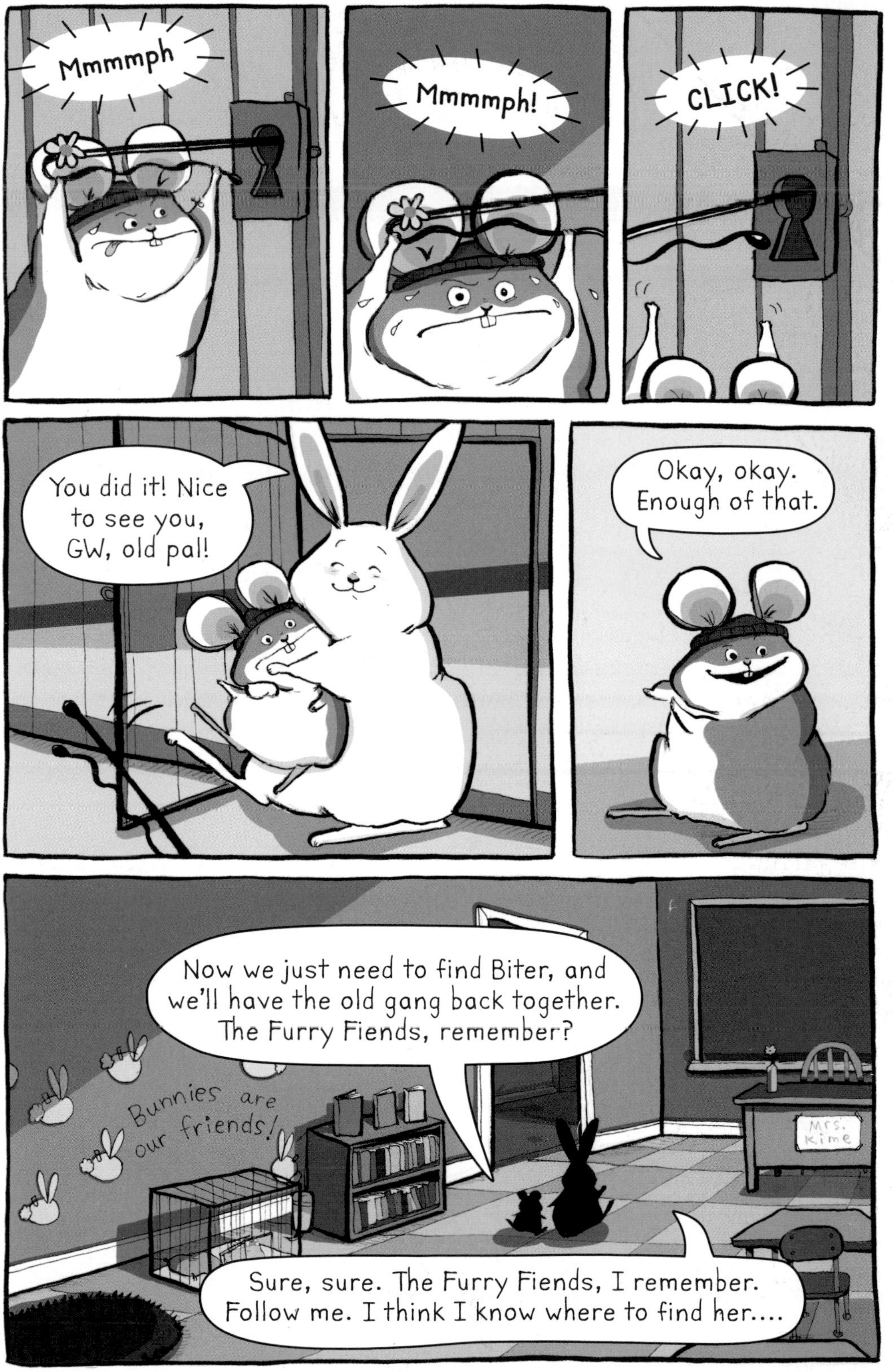
Mmmmph
Mmmmph!
CLICK!
You did it! Nice to see you, GW, old pal!
Okay, okay. Enough of that.
Now we just need to find Biter, and we'll have the old gang back together. The Furry Fiends, remember?
Bunnies are our friends!
Mrs. Kime
Sure, sure. The Furry Fiends, I remember. Follow me. I think I know where to find her....

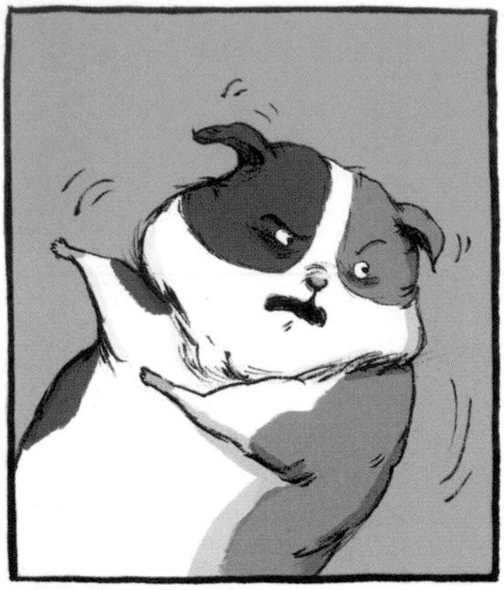

Biter was the toughest, biggest, baddest guinea pig on the planet. Once we found her, everything would be back to normal.

Name: Biter

Species: Guinea pig

Crimes: Do you have another sheet of paper?

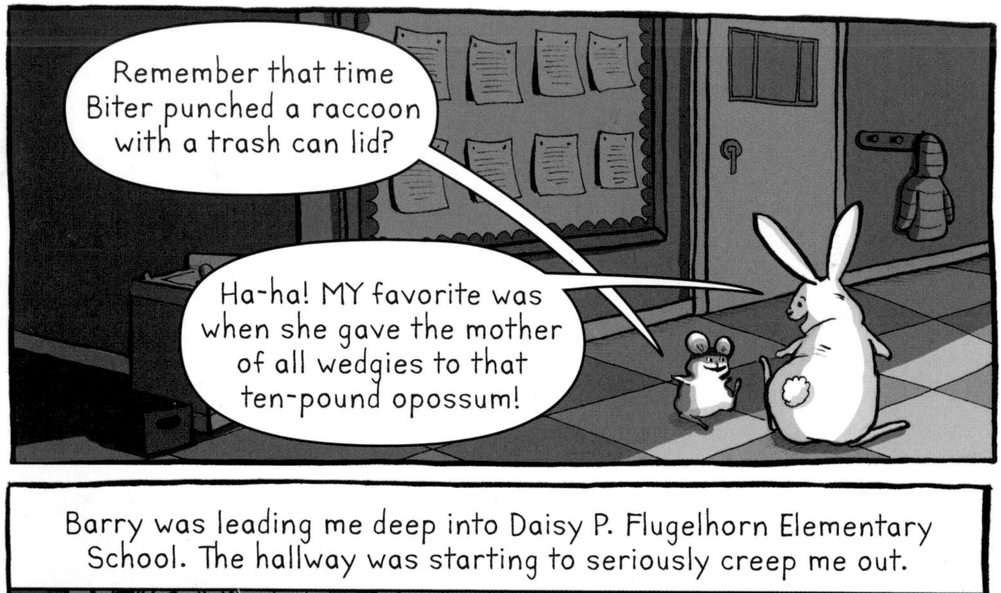

Remember that time Biter punched a raccoon with a trash can lid?
Ha-ha! MY favorite was when she gave the mother of all wedgies to that ten-pound opossum!

Barry was leading me deep into Daisy P. Flugelhorn Elementary School. The hallway was starting to seriously creep me out.

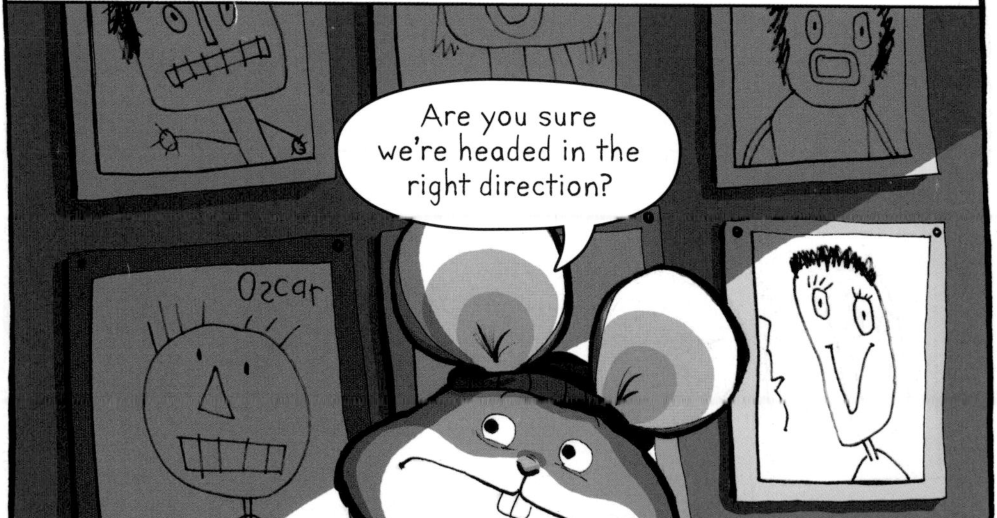

Are you sure we're headed in the right direction?
Oscar

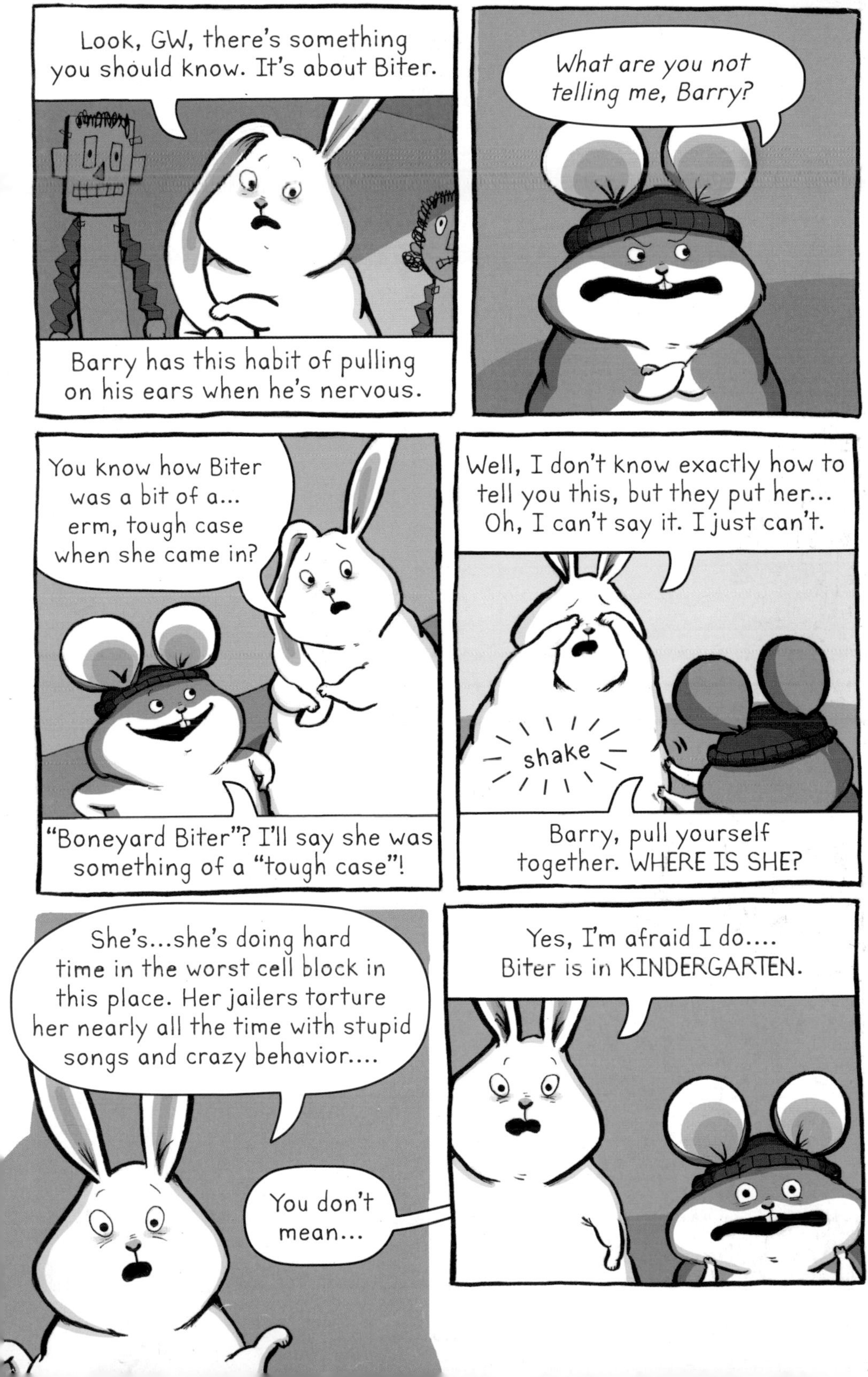

Look, GW, there's something you should know. It's about Biter.
Barry has this habit of pulling on his ears when he's nervous.
What are you not telling me, Barry?
You know how Biter was a bit of a... erm, tough case when she came in?
"Boneyard Biter"? I'll say she was something of a "tough case"!
Well, I don't know exactly how to tell you this, but they put her... Oh, I can't say it. I just can't.
shake
Barry, pull yourself together. WHERE IS SHE?
She's...she's doing hard time in the worst cell block in this place. Her jailers torture her nearly all the time with stupid songs and crazy behavior....
You don't mean...
Yes, I'm afraid I do.... Biter is in KINDERGARTEN.

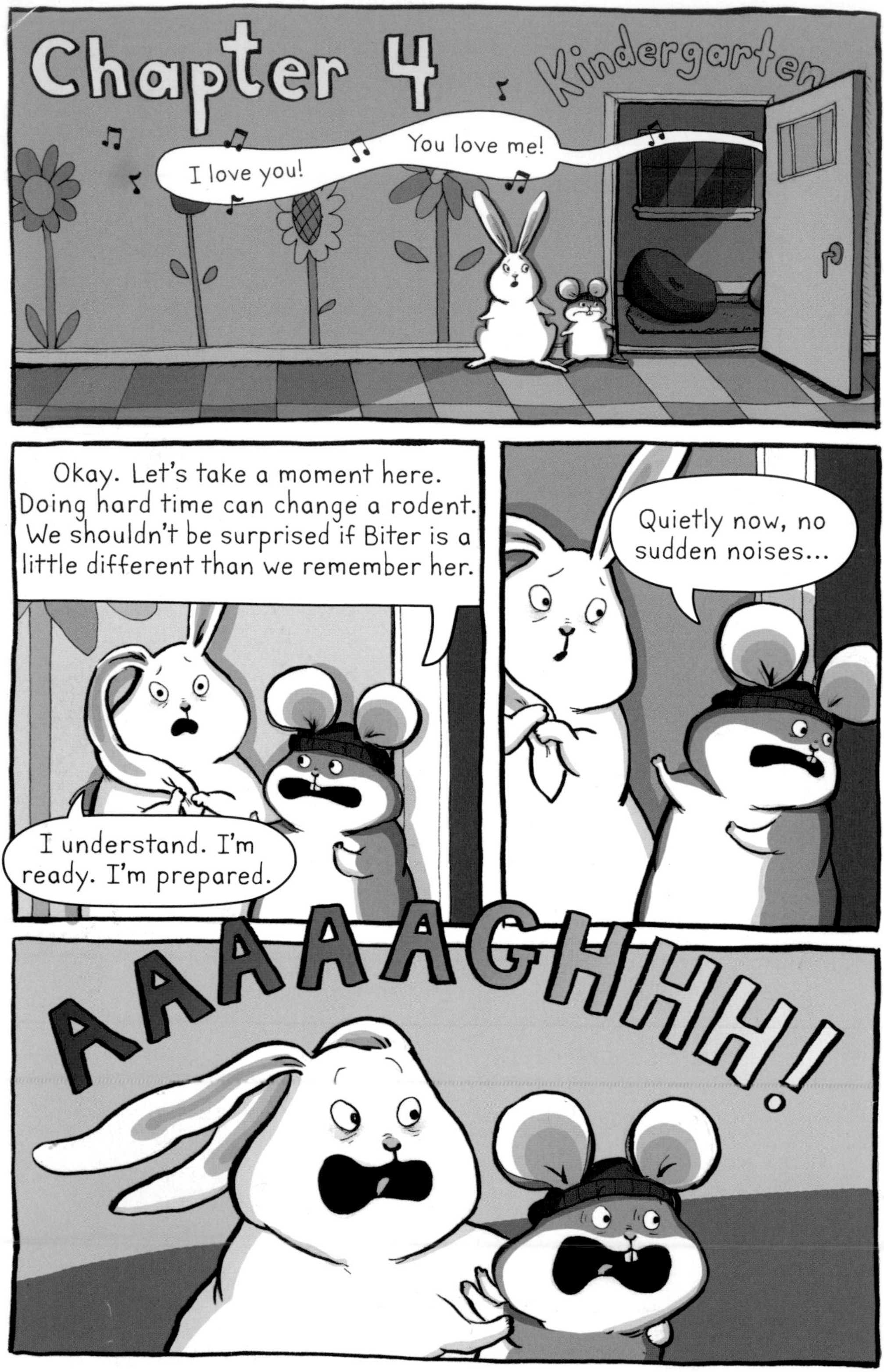

Chapter 4
Kindergarten
I love you!
You love me!
Okay. Let's take a moment here. Doing hard time can change a rodent. We shouldn't be surprised if Biter is a little different than we remember her.
I understand. I'm ready. I'm prepared.
Quietly now, no sudden noises...
AAAAAGHHHH!

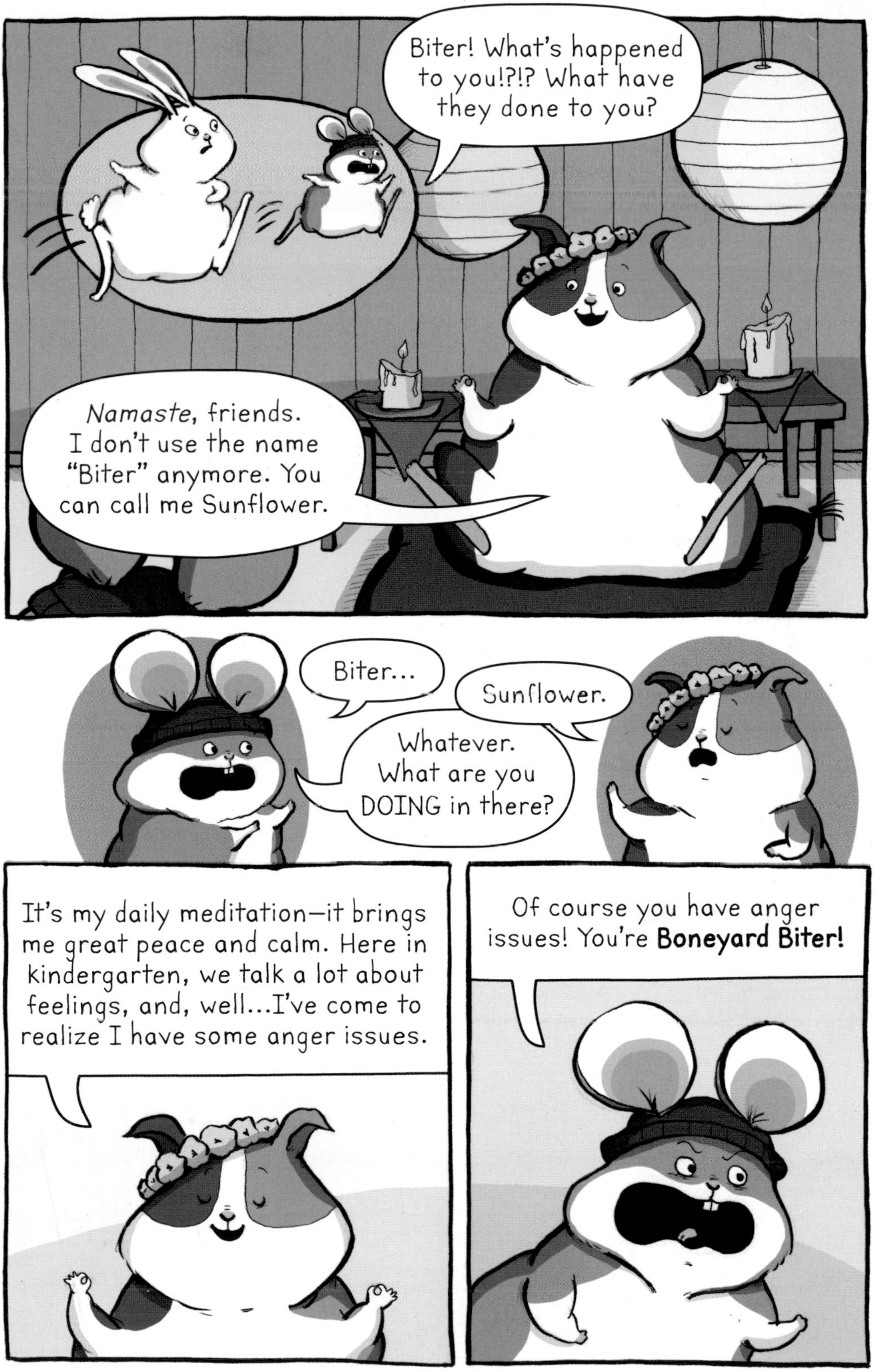
Biter! What's happened to you!?!? What have they done to you?
Namaste, friends. I don't use the name "Biter" anymore. You can call me Sunflower.
Biter...
Sunflower.
Whatever. What are you DOING in there?
It's my daily meditation—it brings me great peace and calm. Here in kindergarten, we talk a lot about feelings, and, well...I've come to realize I have some anger issues.
Of course you have anger issues! You're **Boneyard Biter!**

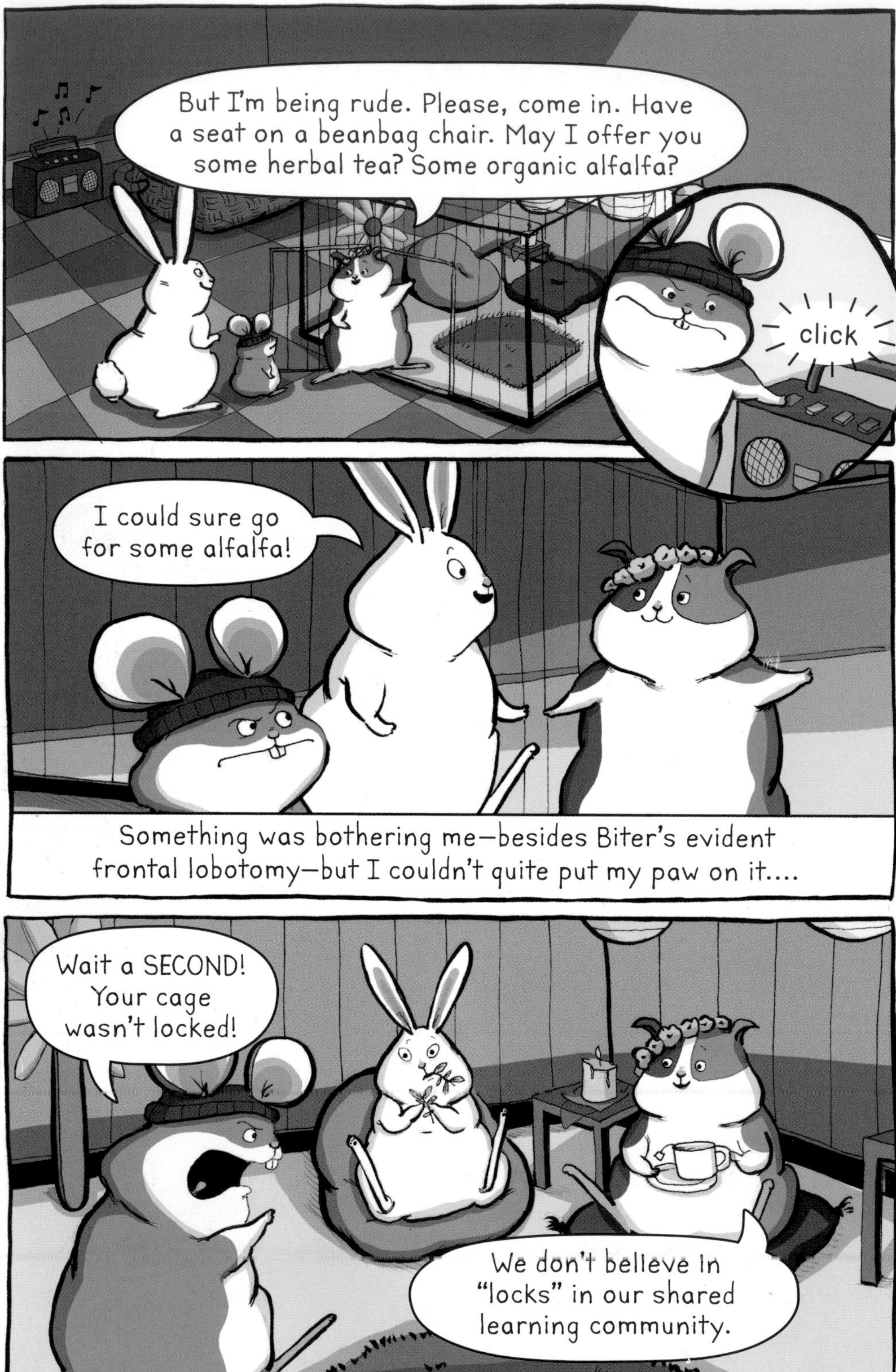
But I'm being rude. Please, come in. Have a seat on a beanbag chair. May I offer you some herbal tea? Some organic alfalfa?
click
I could sure go for some alfalfa!
Something was bothering me—besides Biter's evident frontal lobotomy—but I couldn't quite put my paw on it....
Wait a SECOND! Your cage wasn't locked!
We don't believe in "locks" in our shared learning community.

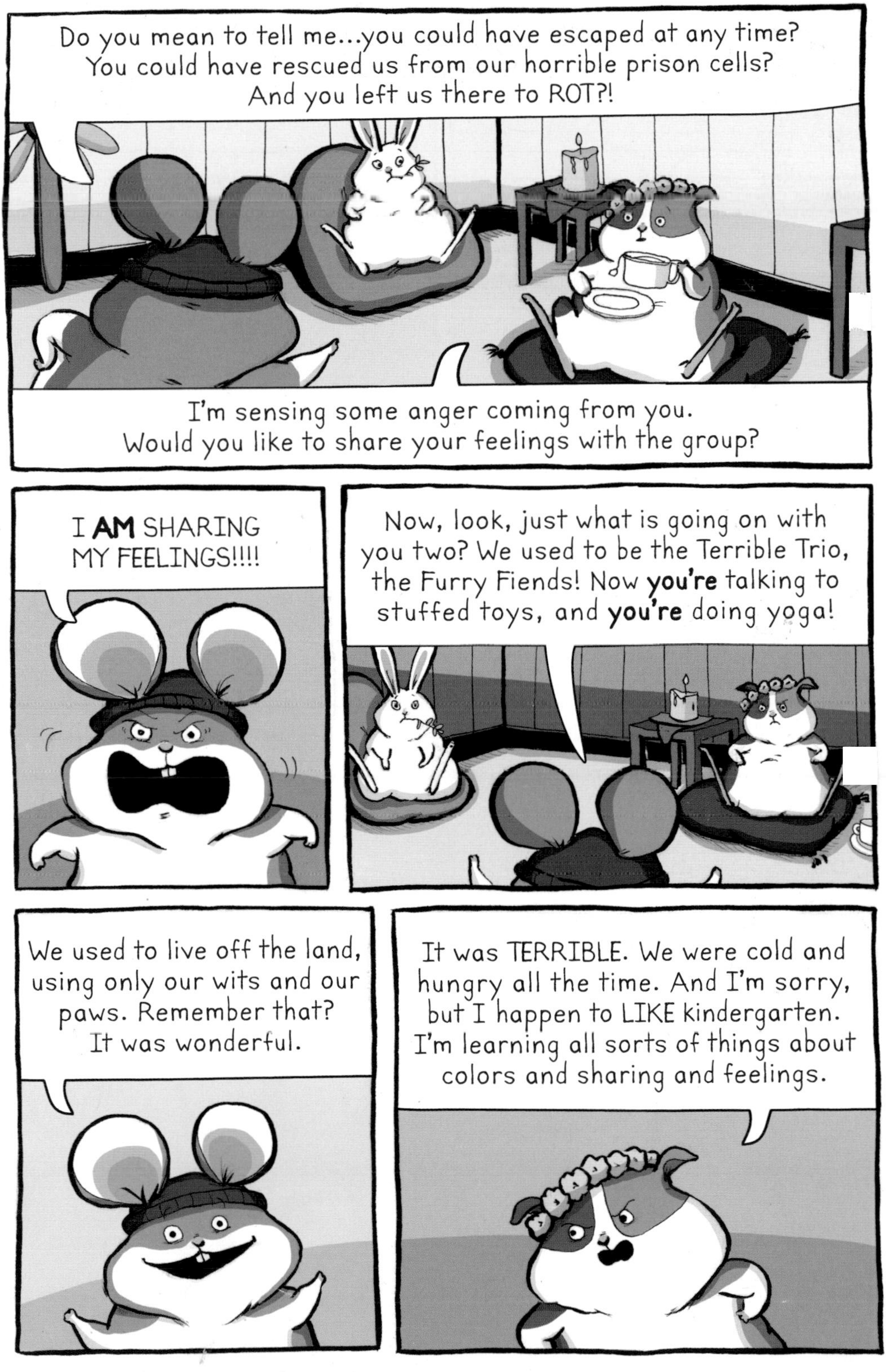
Do you mean to tell me...you could have escaped at any time? You could have rescued us from our horrible prison cells? And you left us there to ROT?!
I'm sensing some anger coming from you. Would you like to share your feelings with the group?
I AM SHARING MY FEELINGS!!!!
Now, look, just what is going on with you two? We used to be the Terrible Trio, the Furry Fiends! Now you're talking to stuffed toys, and you're doing yoga!
We used to live off the land, using only our wits and our paws. Remember that? It was wonderful.
It was TERRIBLE. We were cold and hungry all the time. And I'm sorry, but I happen to LIKE kindergarten. I'm learning all sorts of things about colors and sharing and feelings.

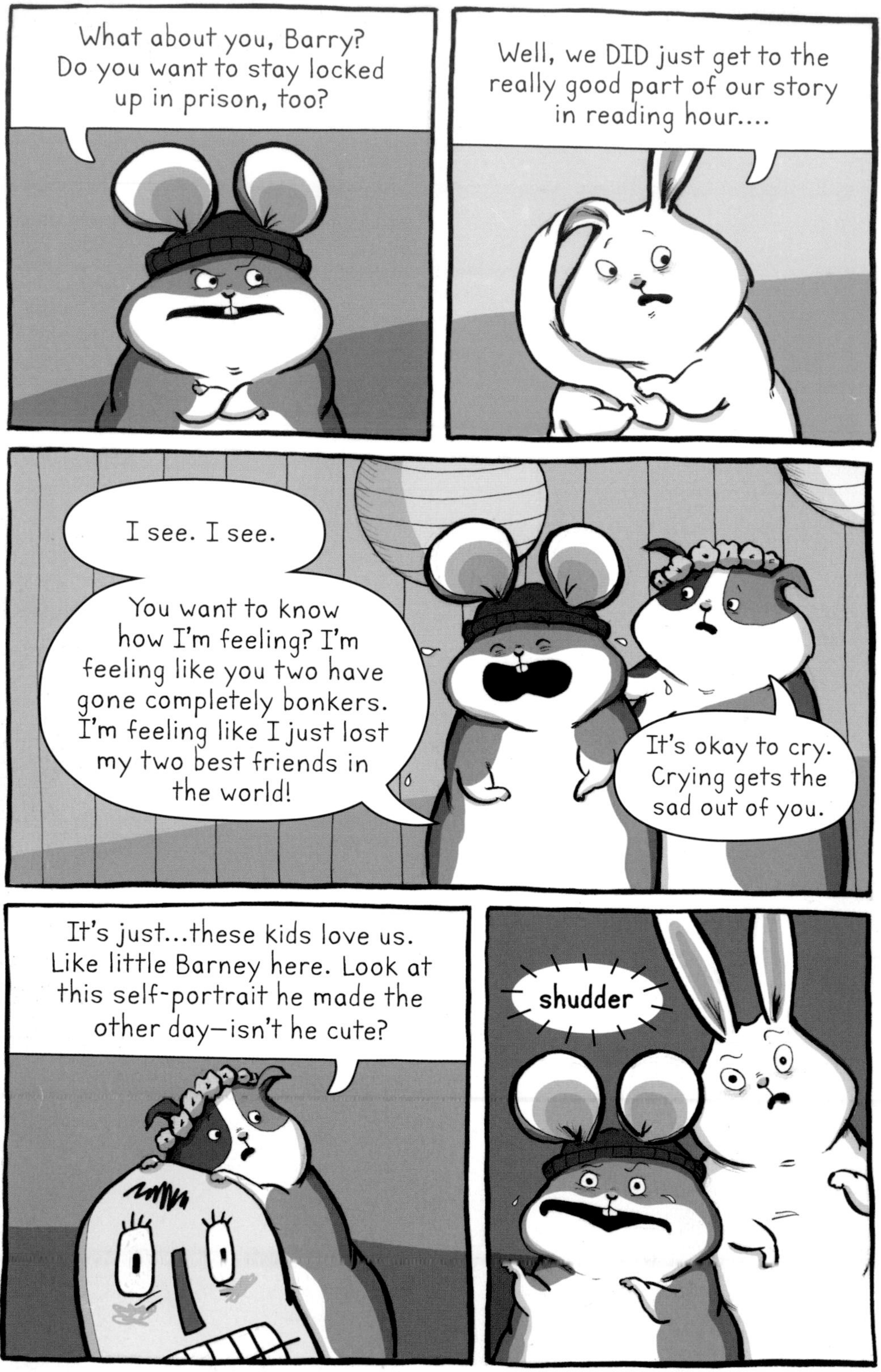
What about you, Barry? Do you want to stay locked up in prison, too?
Well, we DID just get to the really good part of our story in reading hour....
I see. I see.
You want to know how I'm feeling? I'm feeling like you two have gone completely bonkers. I'm feeling like I just lost my two best friends in the world!
It's okay to cry. Crying gets the sad out of you.
It's just...these kids love us. Like little Barney here. Look at this self-portrait he made the other day—isn't he cute?
shudder

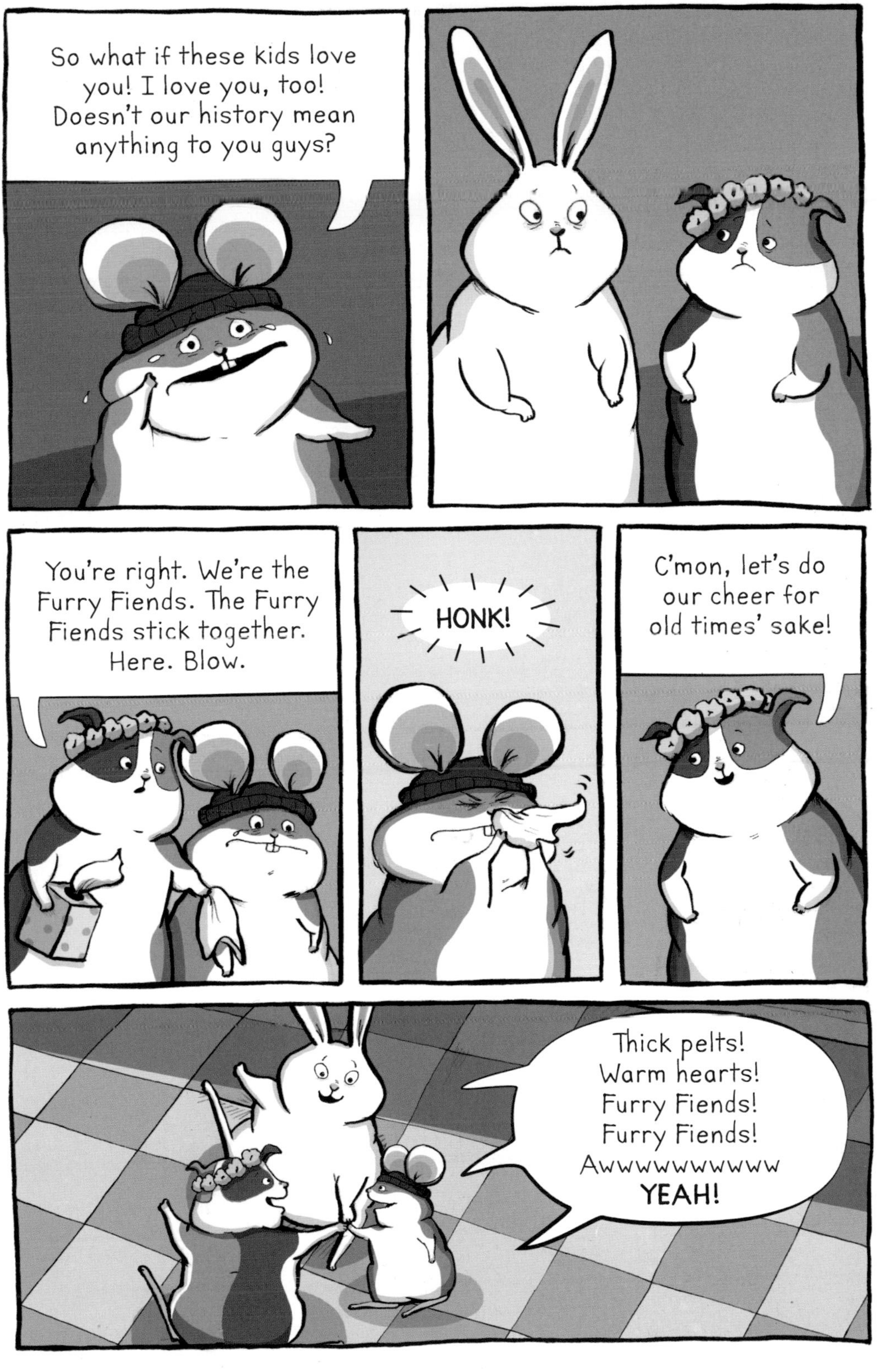
So what if these kids love you! I love you, too! Doesn't our history mean anything to you guys?
You're right. We're the Furry Fiends. The Furry Fiends stick together. Here. Blow.
HONK!
C'mon, let's do our cheer for old times' sake!
Thick pelts! Warm hearts! Furry Fiends! Furry Fiends! Awwwwwwwwww **YEAH!**

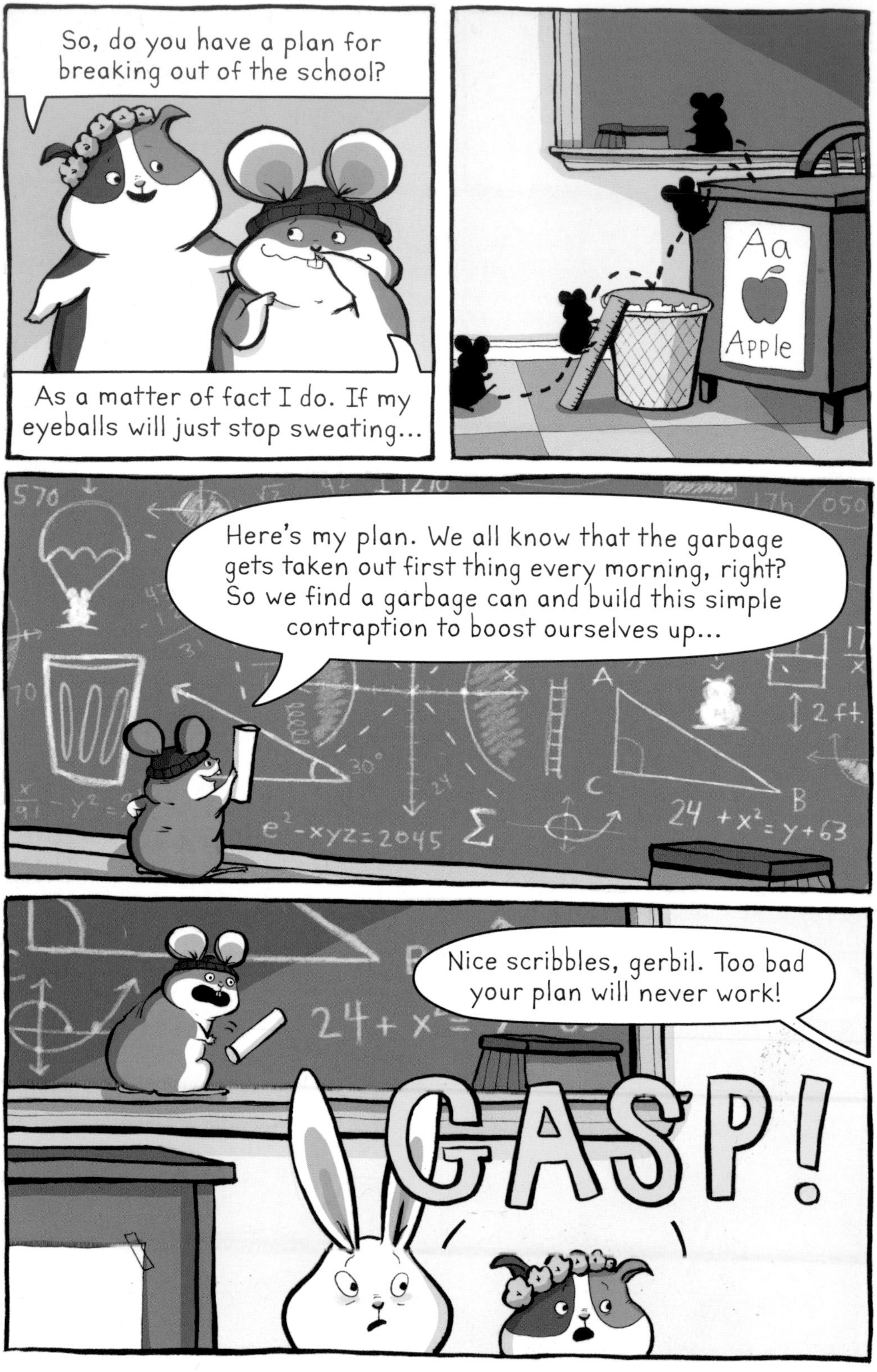
So, do you have a plan for breaking out of the school?
As a matter of fact I do. If my eyeballs will just stop sweating...
Aa
Apple
Here's my plan. We all know that the garbage gets taken out first thing every morning, right? So we find a garbage can and build this simple contraption to boost ourselves up...
Nice scribbles, gerbil. Too bad your plan will never work!
GASP!

Chapter 5

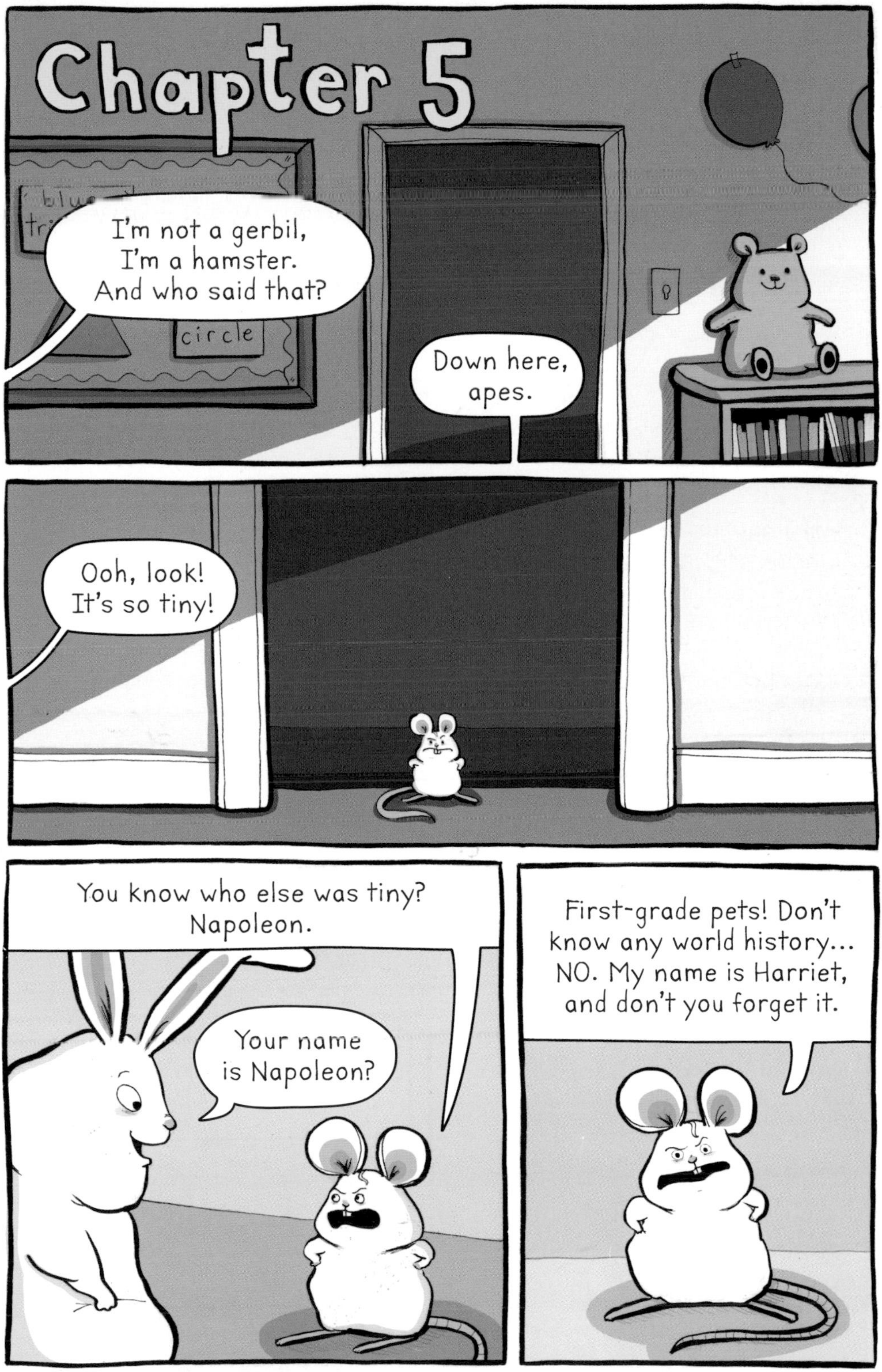

blue
tri
circle
I'm not a gerbil, I'm a hamster. And who said that?
Down here, apes.
Ooh, look! It's so tiny!
You know who else was tiny? Napoleon.
Your name is Napoleon?
First-grade pets! Don't know any world history... NO. My name is Harriet, and don't you forget it.

Before you go on with your big escape plans, let me explain how things work here in Daisy P. Flugelhorn Elementary School. I'm a fourth-grade pet, which means I have seniority over you.

"Seniority," for those of you with a preschool reading level, means I get to tell you what to do.

And **I** say, no one is breaking out of this school. When class pets break loose, that means tighter security. And Harriet doesn't LIKE tighter security. Harriet likes to roam around the school at night, creating mischief and mayhem wherever she goes!

And Harriet is going to stop us from breaking out?

I is...I mean, she... I mean, Harriet...yes.

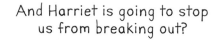

Oh yeah? Harriet and what army?

I am so glad you asked.

26

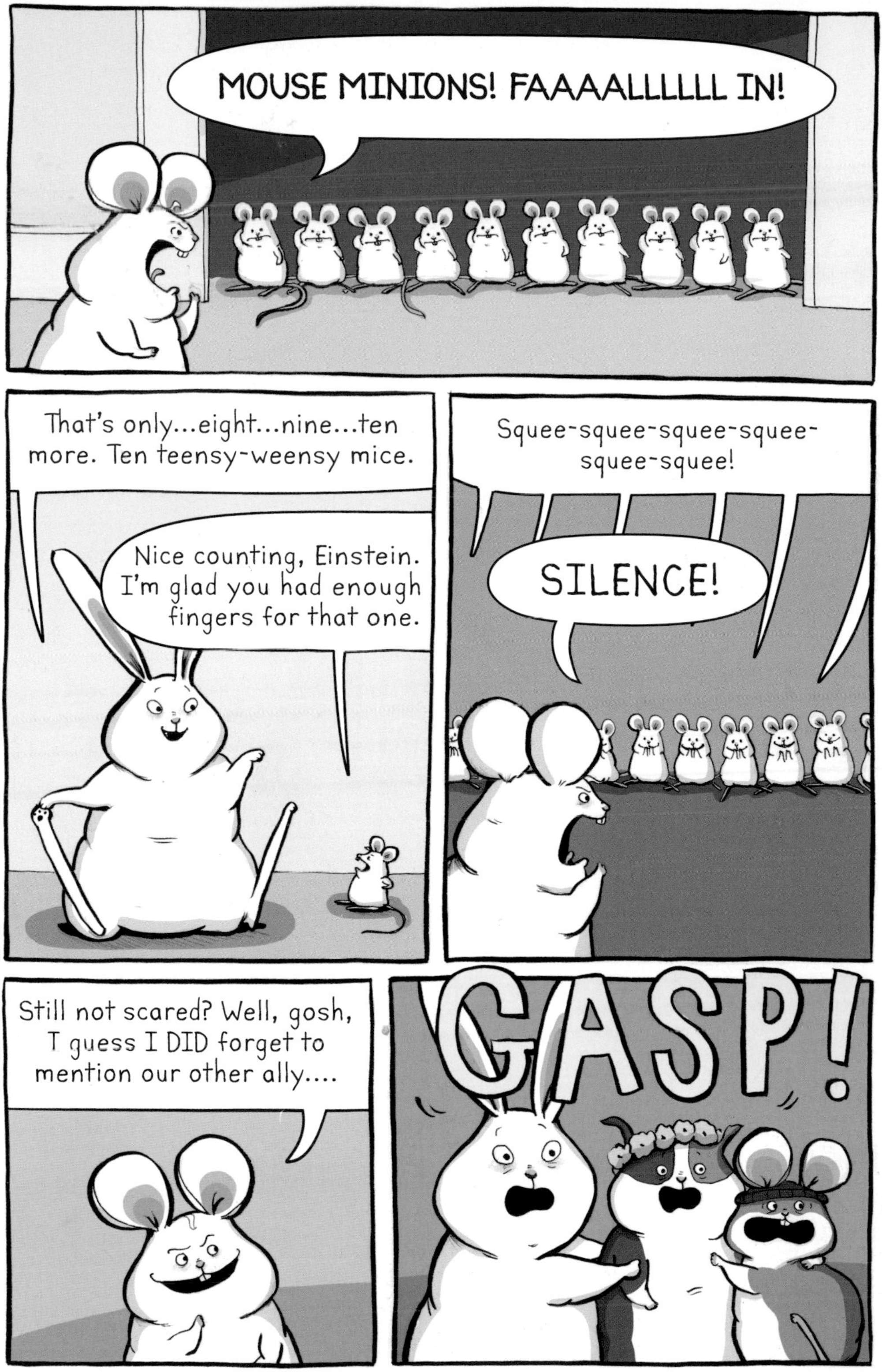
MOUSE MINIONS! FAAAALLLLLL IN!
That's only...eight...nine...ten more. Ten teensy-weensy mice.
Nice counting, Einstein. I'm glad you had enough fingers for that one.
Squee-squee-squee-squee-squee-squee!
SILENCE!
Still not scared? Well, gosh, I guess I DID forget to mention our other ally....
GASP!

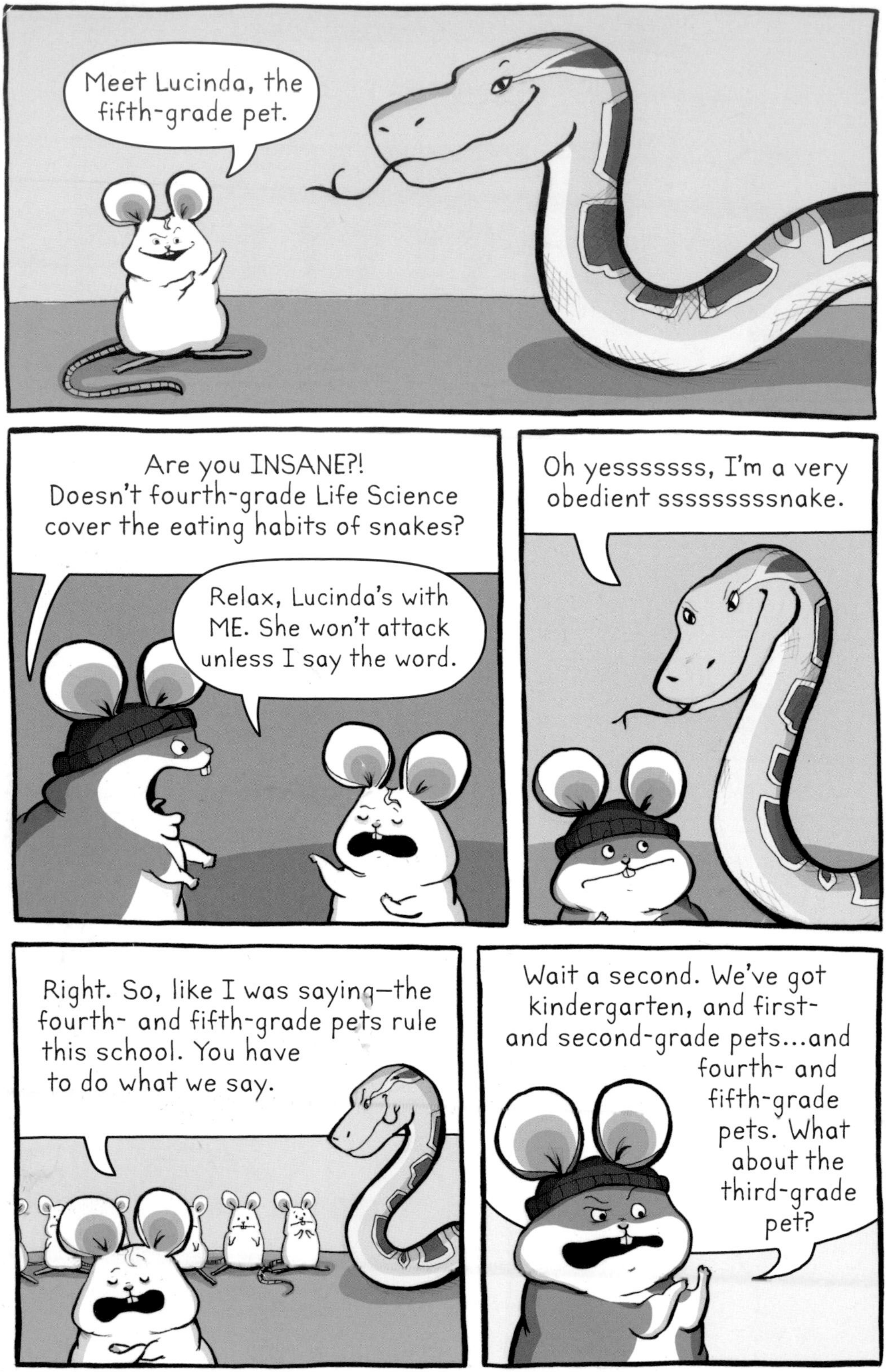
Meet Lucinda, the fifth-grade pet.
Are you INSANE?! Doesn't fourth-grade Life Science cover the eating habits of snakes?
Relax, Lucinda's with ME. She won't attack unless I say the word.
Oh yesssssss, I'm a very obedient sssssssssnake.
Right. So, like I was saying—the fourth- and fifth-grade pets rule this school. You have to do what we say.
Wait a second. We've got kindergarten, and first- and second-grade pets...and fourth- and fifth-grade pets. What about the third-grade pet?

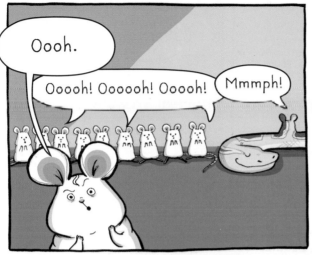

Oooh.

Ooooh! Ooooooh! Ooooh!

Mmmph!

The third graders in this school are so horrible, SO rotten... they're NOT ALLOWED TO HAVE A PET.

Is this awkward silence over now? Because we'd like to get going.

Not so fast, rat.

HAMSTER!

Mouse Minions, put these three in lockdown!

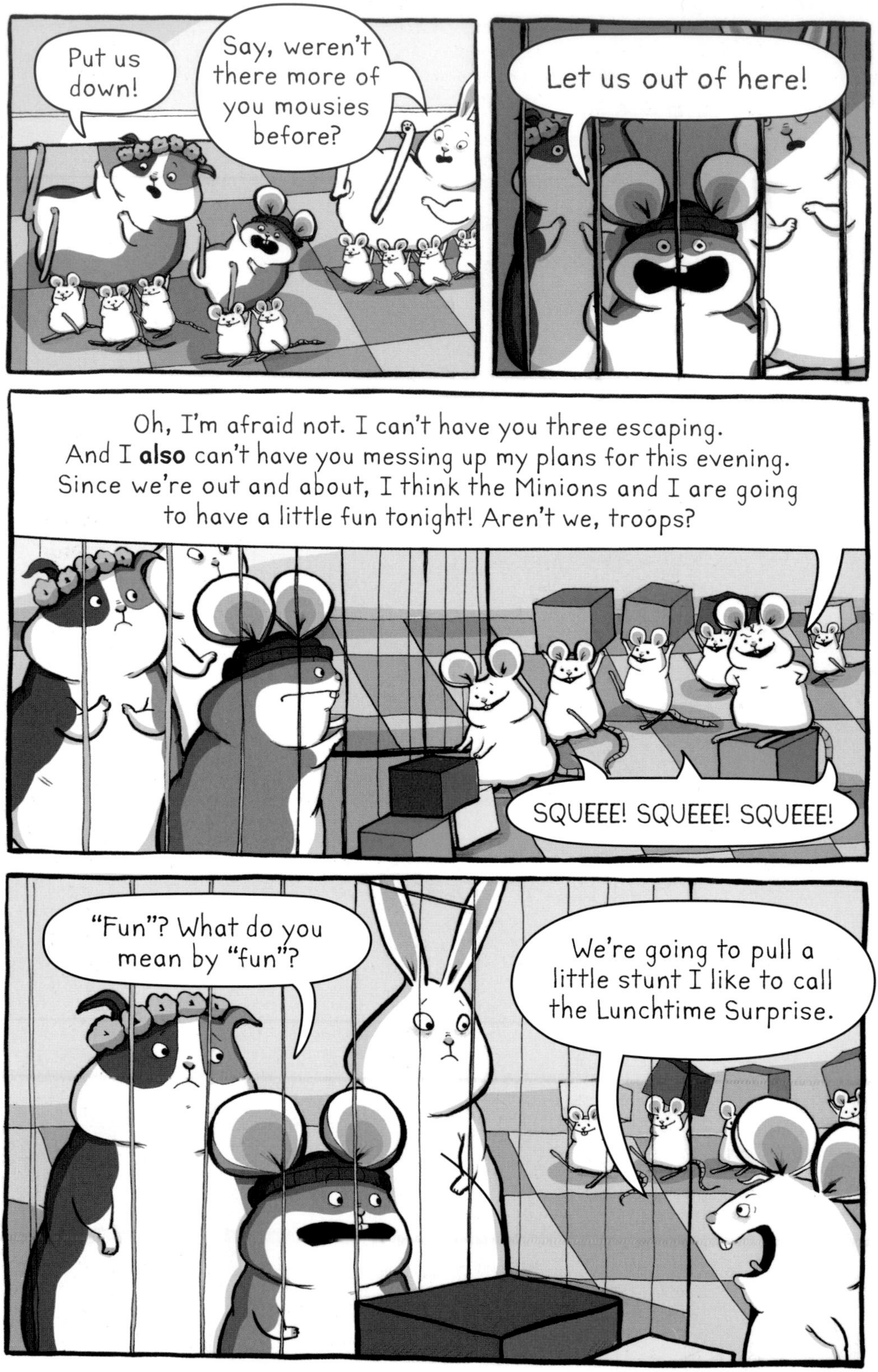
Put us down!
Say, weren't there more of you mousies before?
Let us out of here!
Oh, I'm afraid not. I can't have you three escaping. And I **also** can't have you messing up my plans for this evening. Since we're out and about, I think the Minions and I are going to have a little fun tonight! Aren't we, troops?
SQUEEE! SQUEEE! SQUEEE!
"Fun"? What do you mean by "fun"?
We're going to pull a little stunt I like to call the Lunchtime Surprise.

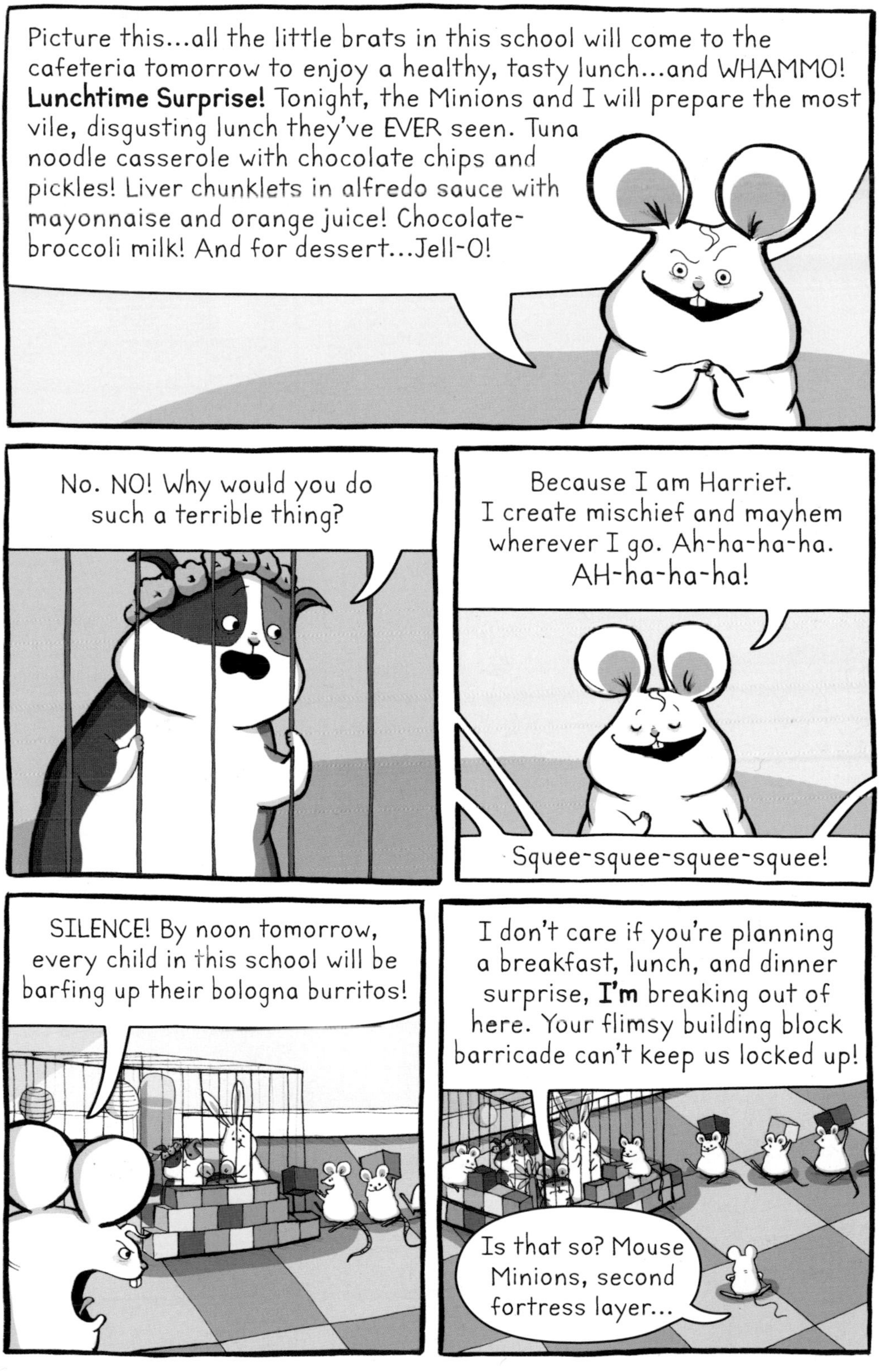

Picture this...all the little brats in this school will come to the cafeteria tomorrow to enjoy a healthy, tasty lunch...and WHAMMO! **Lunchtime Surprise!** Tonight, the Minions and I will prepare the most vile, disgusting lunch they've EVER seen. Tuna noodle casserole with chocolate chips and pickles! Liver chunklets in alfredo sauce with mayonnaise and orange juice! Chocolate-broccoli milk! And for dessert...Jell-O!
No. NO! Why would you do such a terrible thing?
Because I am Harriet. I create mischief and mayhem wherever I go. Ah-ha-ha-ha. AH-ha-ha-ha!
Squee-squee-squee-squee!
SILENCE! By noon tomorrow, every child in this school will be barfing up their bologna burritos!
I don't care if you're planning a breakfast, lunch, and dinner surprise, **I'm** breaking out of here. Your flimsy building block barricade can't keep us locked up!
Is that so? Mouse Minions, second fortress layer...

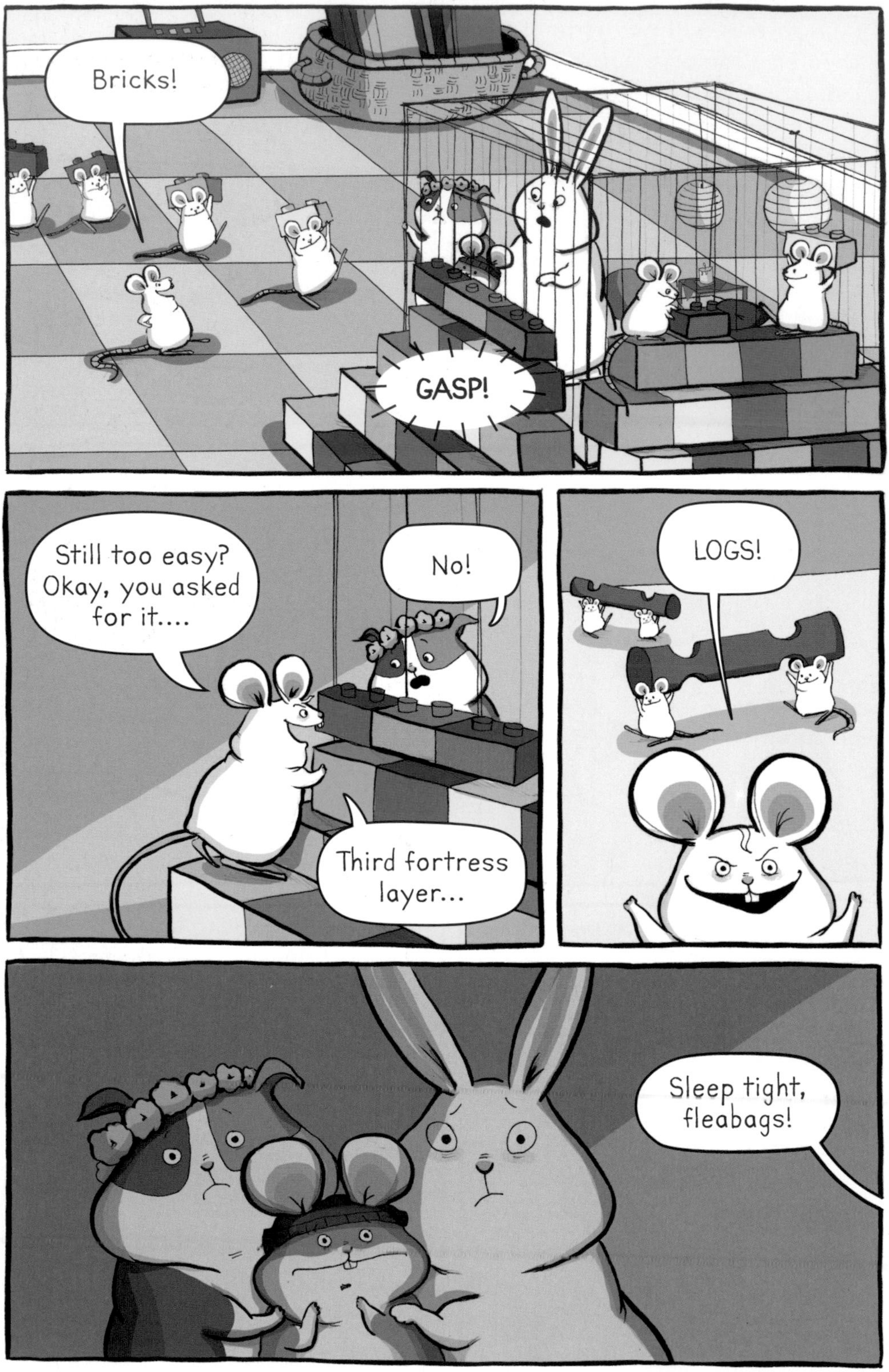
Bricks!
GASP!
Still too easy? Okay, you asked for it....
No!
Third fortress layer...
LOGS!
Sleep tight, fleabags!

Chapter 6

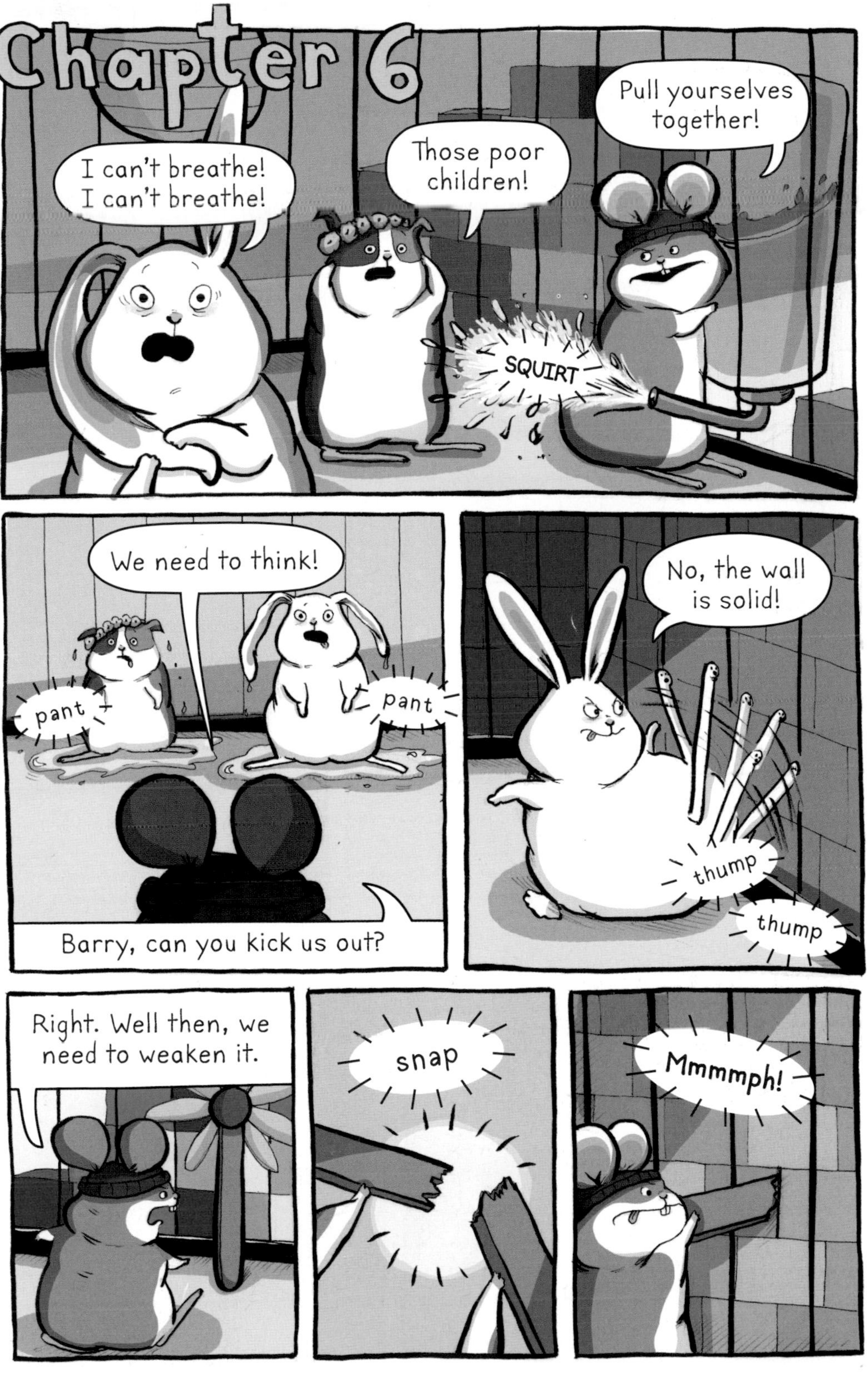

I can't breathe!
I can't breathe!
Those poor children!
Pull yourselves together!
SQUIRT
We need to think!
pant
pant
Barry, can you kick us out?
No, the wall is solid!
thump
thump
Right. Well then, we need to weaken it.
snap
Mmmmph!

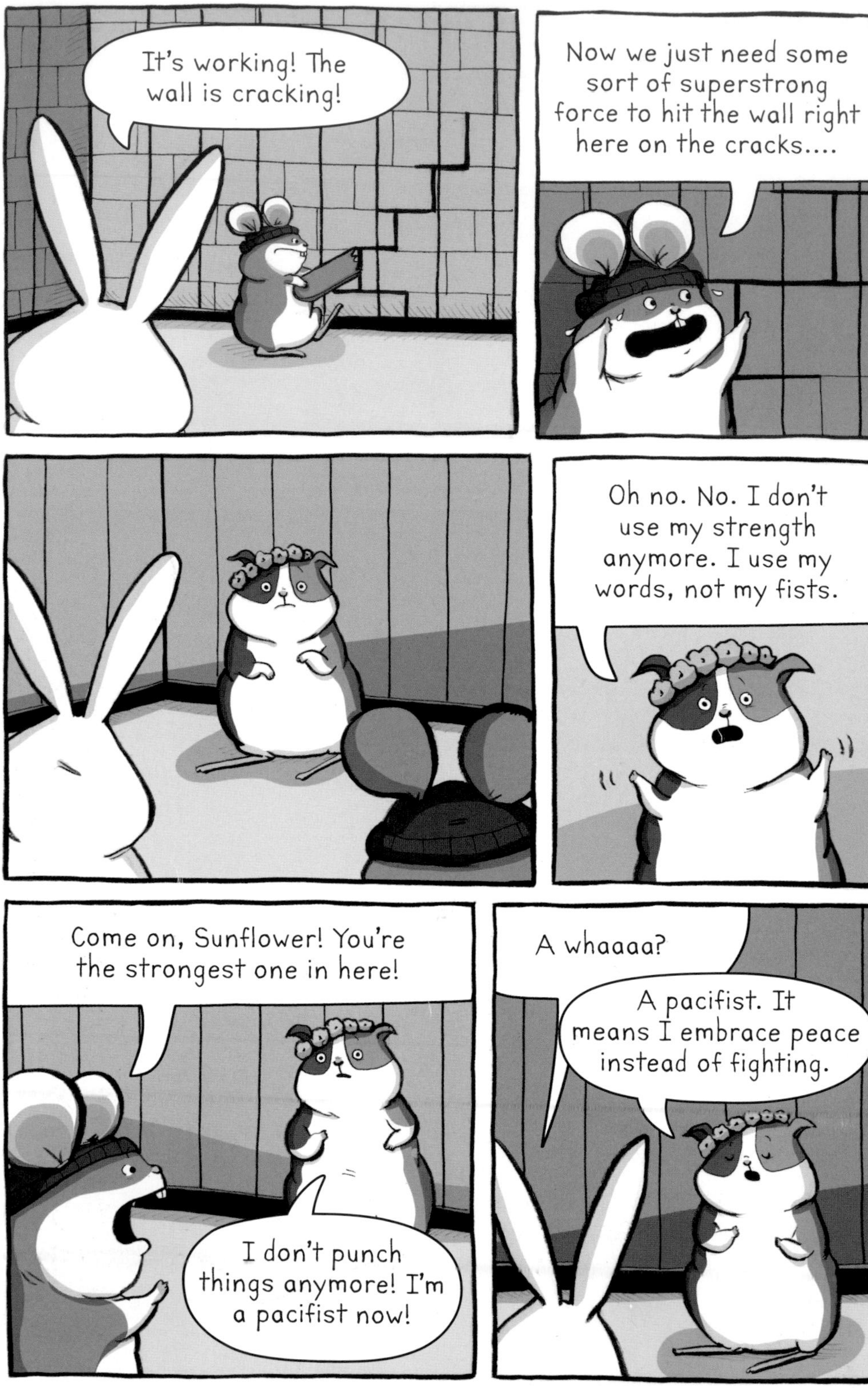
It's working! The wall is cracking!
Now we just need some sort of superstrong force to hit the wall right here on the cracks....
Oh no. No. I don't use my strength anymore. I use my words, not my fists.
Come on, Sunflower! You're the strongest one in here!
I don't punch things anymore! I'm a pacifist now!
A whaaaa?
A pacifist. It means I embrace peace instead of fighting.

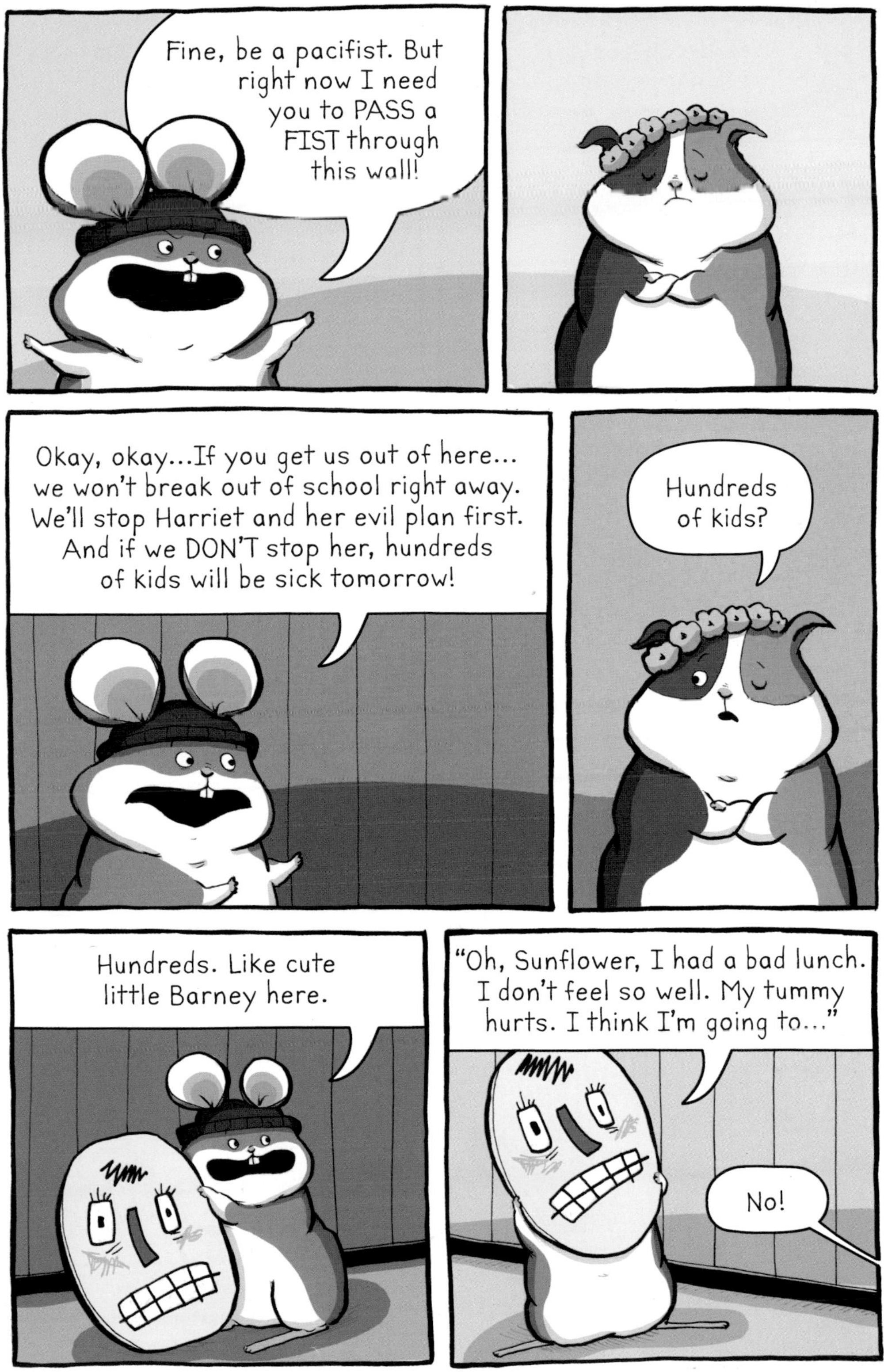
Fine, be a pacifist. But right now I need you to PASS a FIST through this wall!
Okay, okay...If you get us out of here... we won't break out of school right away. We'll stop Harriet and her evil plan first. And if we DON'T stop her, hundreds of kids will be sick tomorrow!
Hundreds of kids?
Hundreds. Like cute little Barney here.
"Oh, Sunflower, I had a bad lunch. I don't feel so well. My tummy hurts. I think I'm going to..."
No!

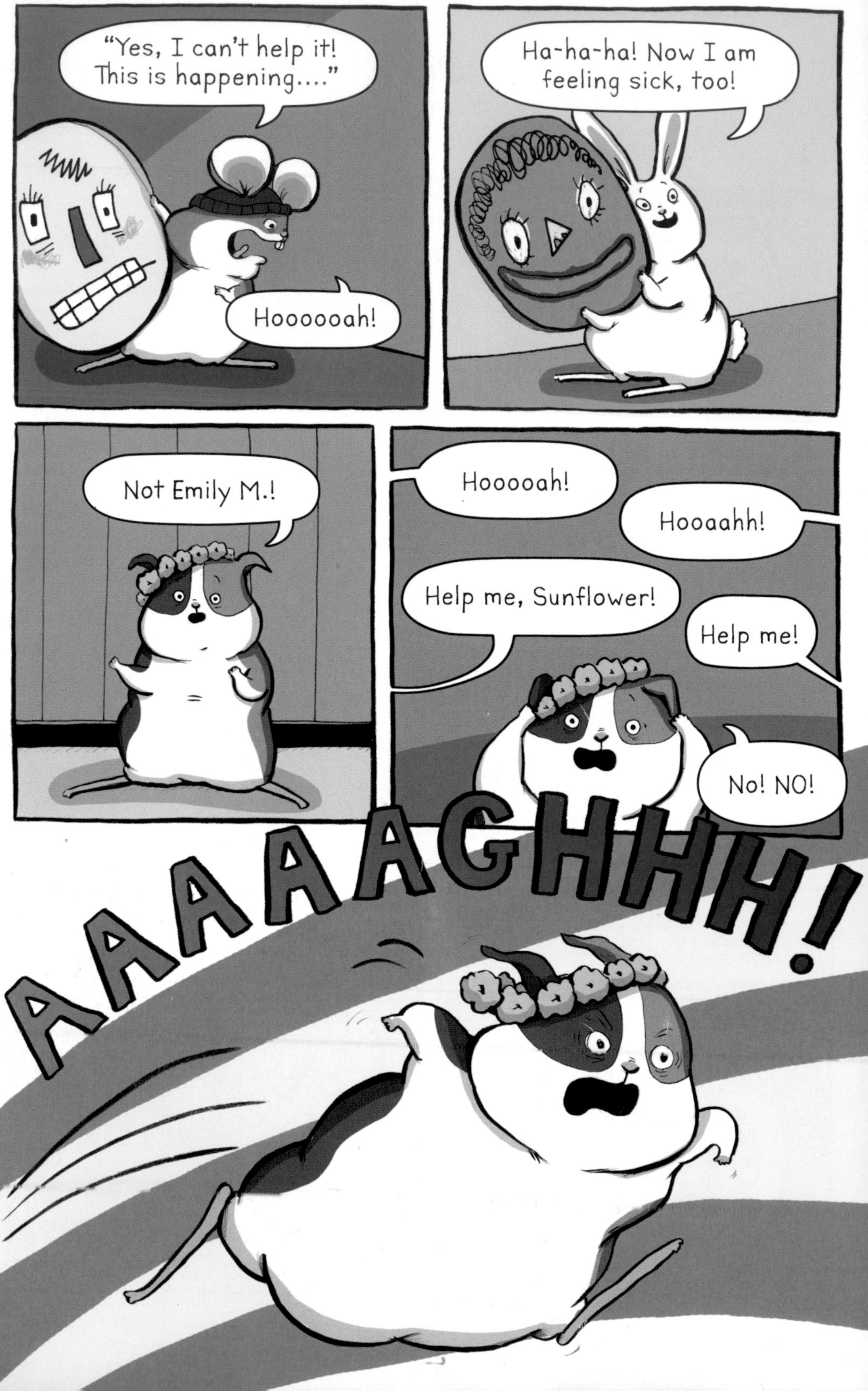
"Yes, I can't help it! This is happening...."
Hoooooah!
Ha-ha-ha! Now I am feeling sick, too!
Not Emily M.!
Hooooah!
Hooaahh!
Help me, Sunflower!
Help me!
No! NO!
AAAAAGHHH!

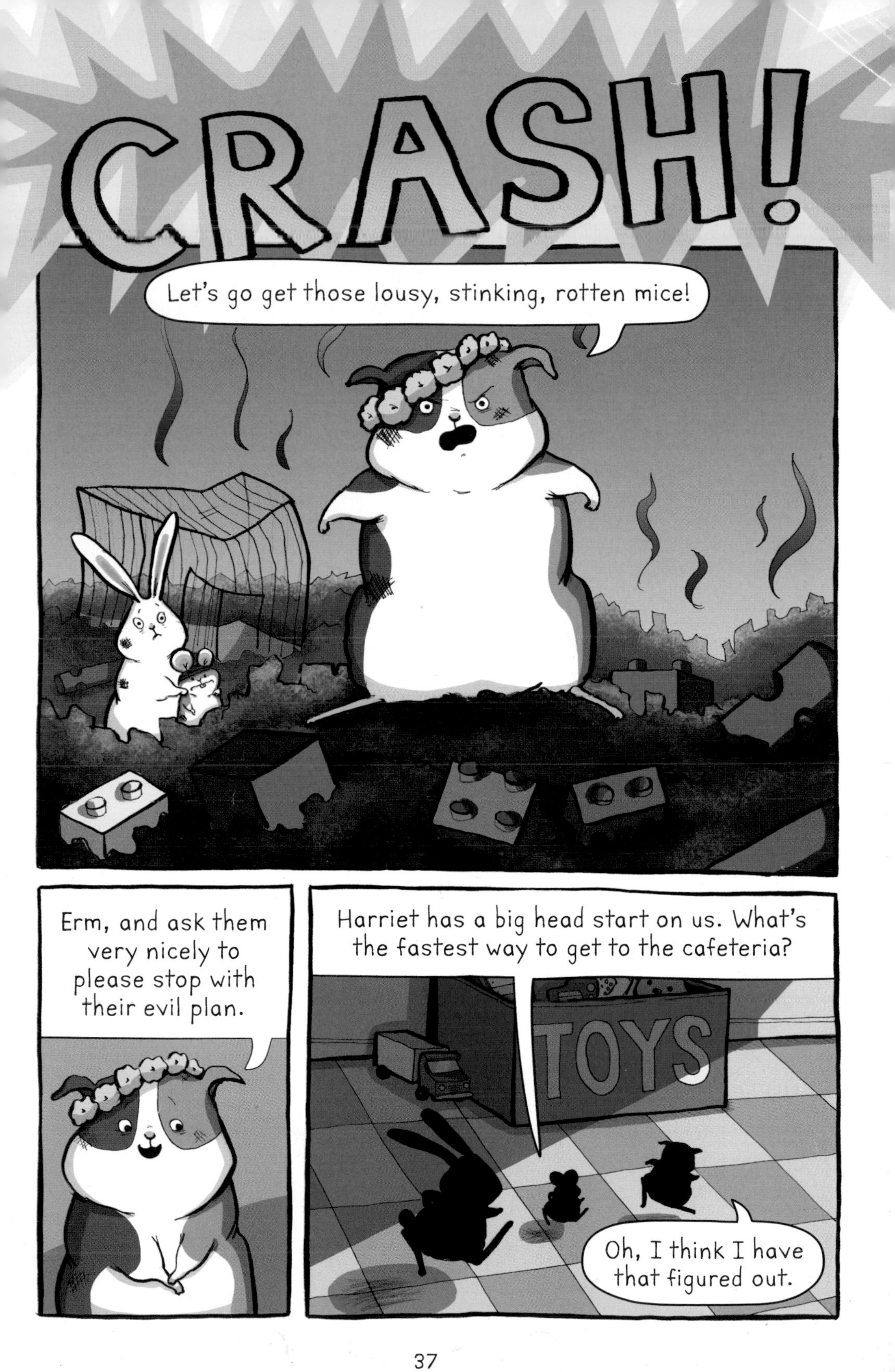
CRASH!
Let's go get those lousy, stinking, rotten mice!
Erm, and ask them very nicely to please stop with their evil plan.
Harriet has a big head start on us. What's the fastest way to get to the cafeteria?
TOYS
Oh, I think I have that figured out.

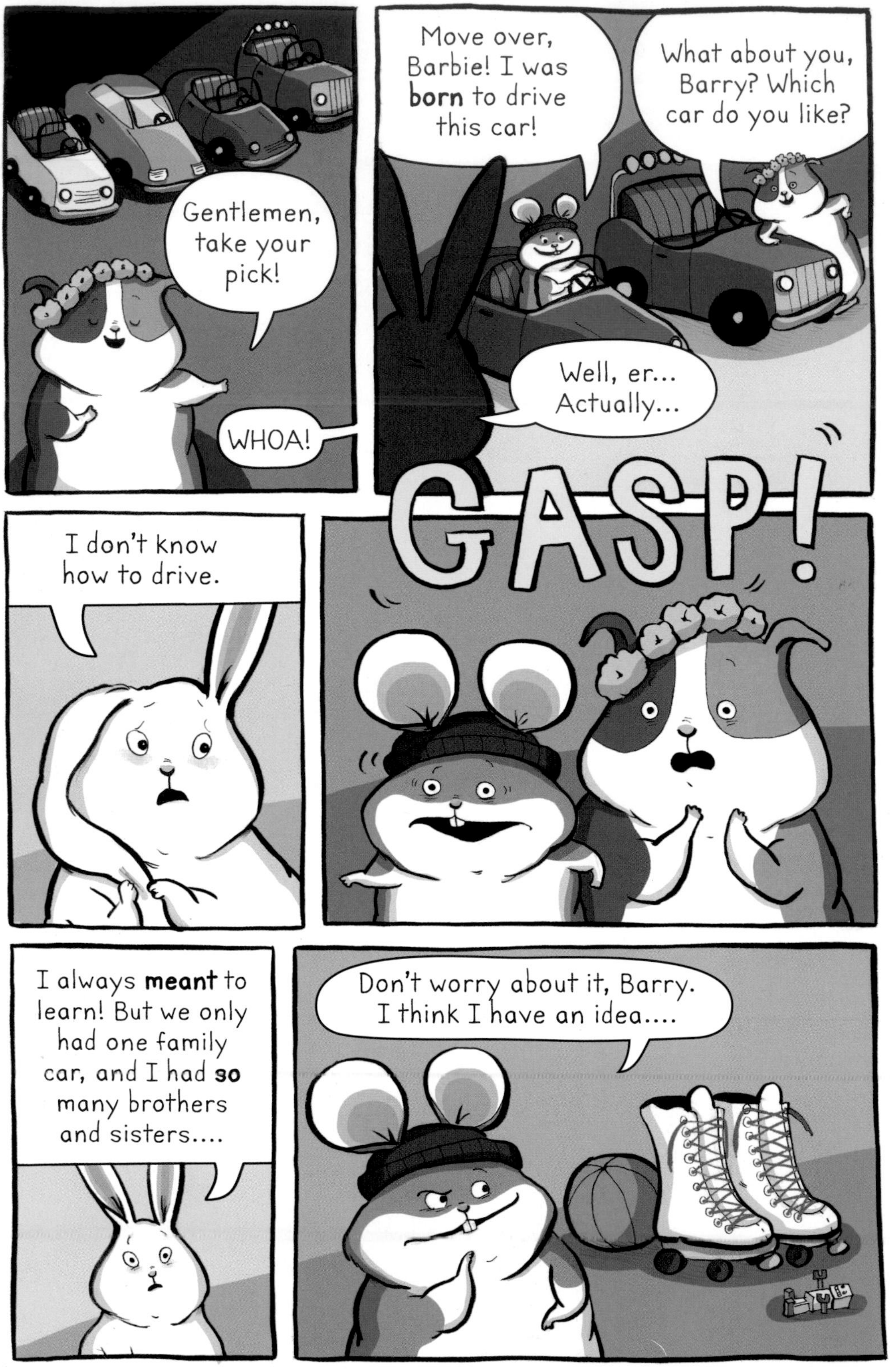
Gentlemen, take your pick!
WHOA!
Move over, Barbie! I was **born** to drive this car!
What about you, Barry? Which car do you like?
Well, er... Actually...
GASP!
I don't know how to drive.
I always **meant** to learn! But we only had one family car, and I had **so** many brothers and sisters....
Don't worry about it, Barry. I think I have an idea....

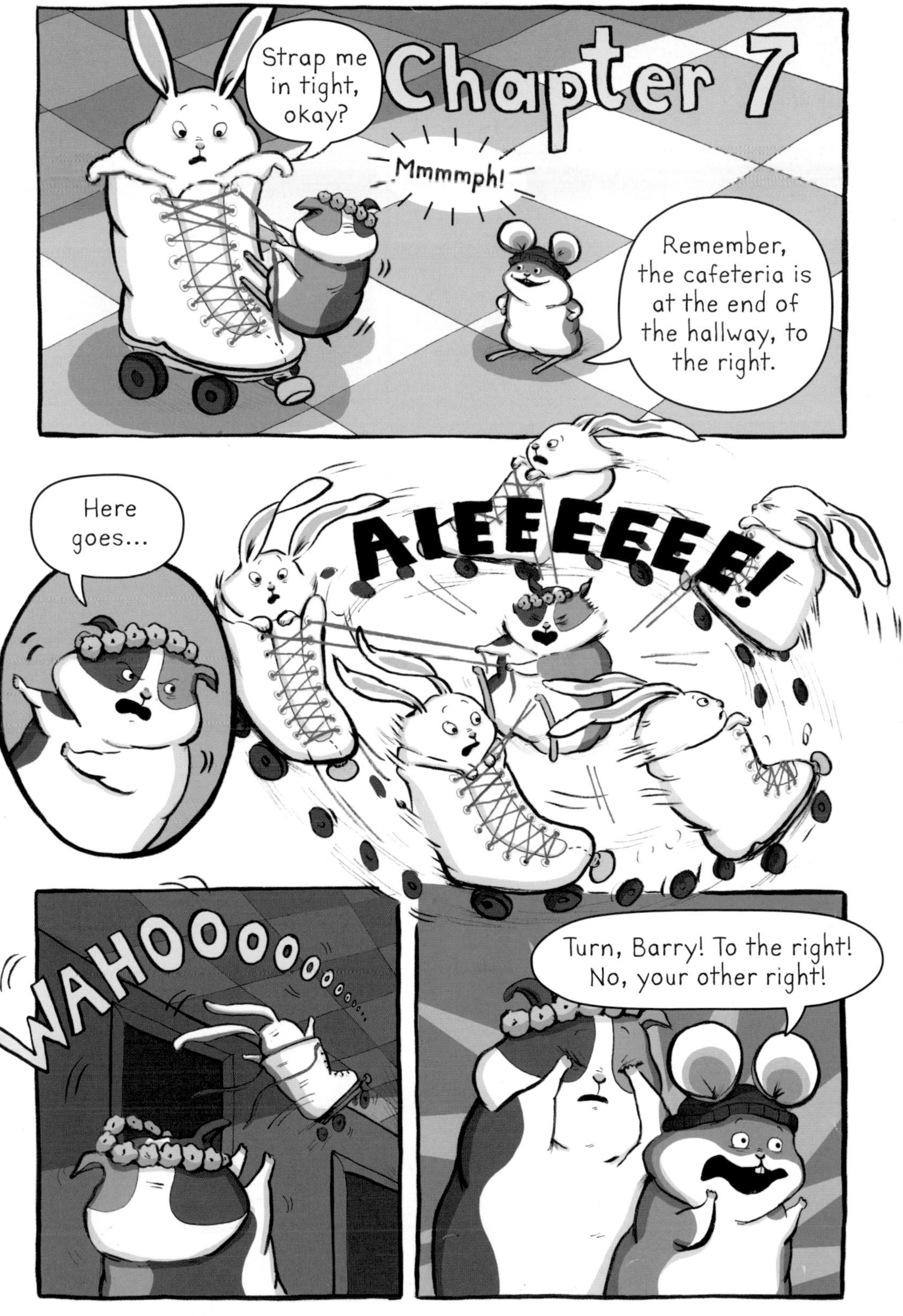
Chapter 7
Strap me in tight, okay?
Mmmmph!
Remember, the cafeteria is at the end of the hallway, to the right.
Here goes...
AIEEEEEEE!
WAHOOOOOooooo...
Turn, Barry! To the right! No, your other right!

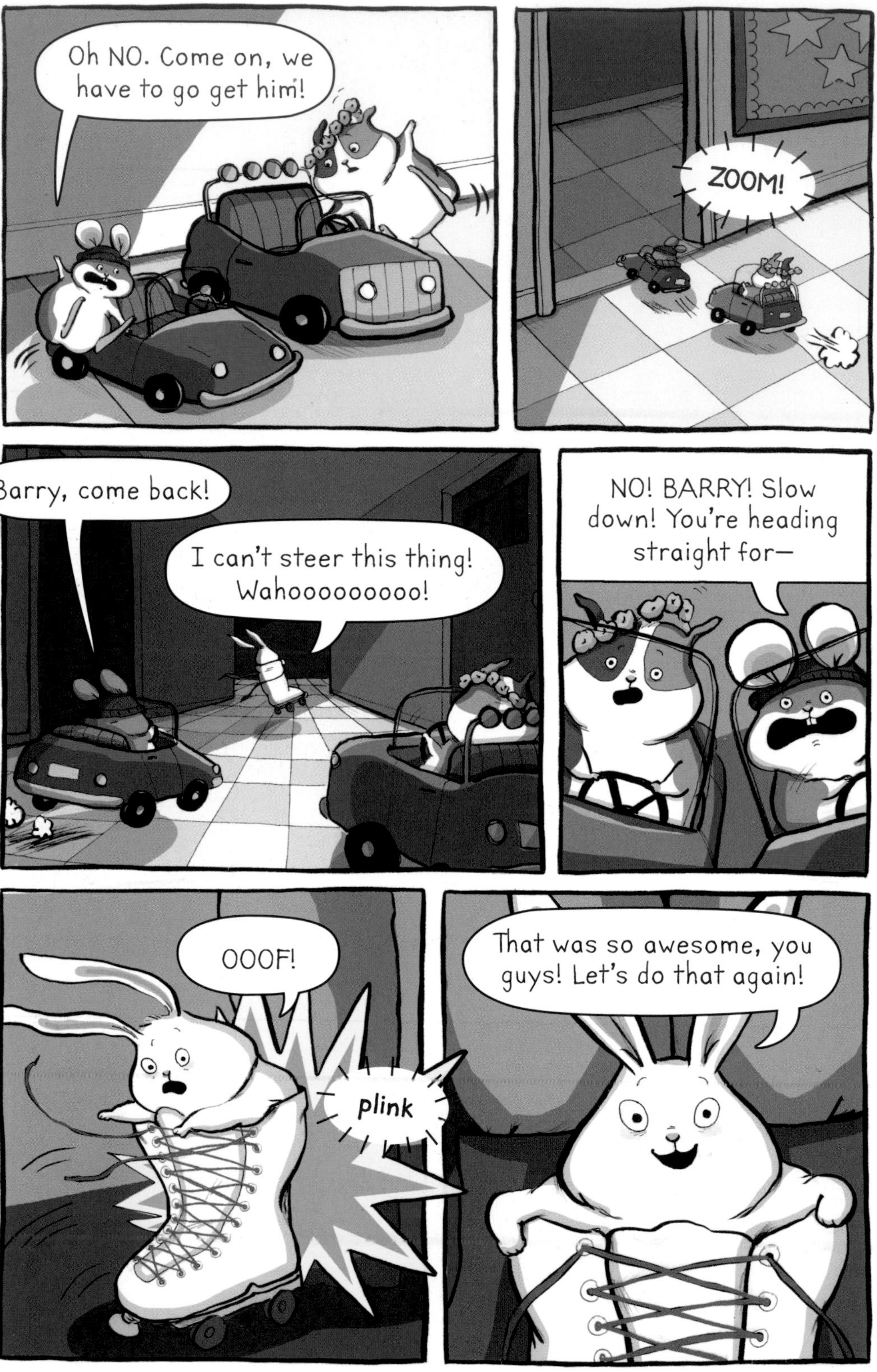

Oh NO. Come on, we have to go get him!
ZOOM!
Barry, come back!
I can't steer this thing! Wahoooooooooo!
NO! BARRY! Slow down! You're heading straight for—
OOOF!
plink
That was so awesome, you guys! Let's do that again!

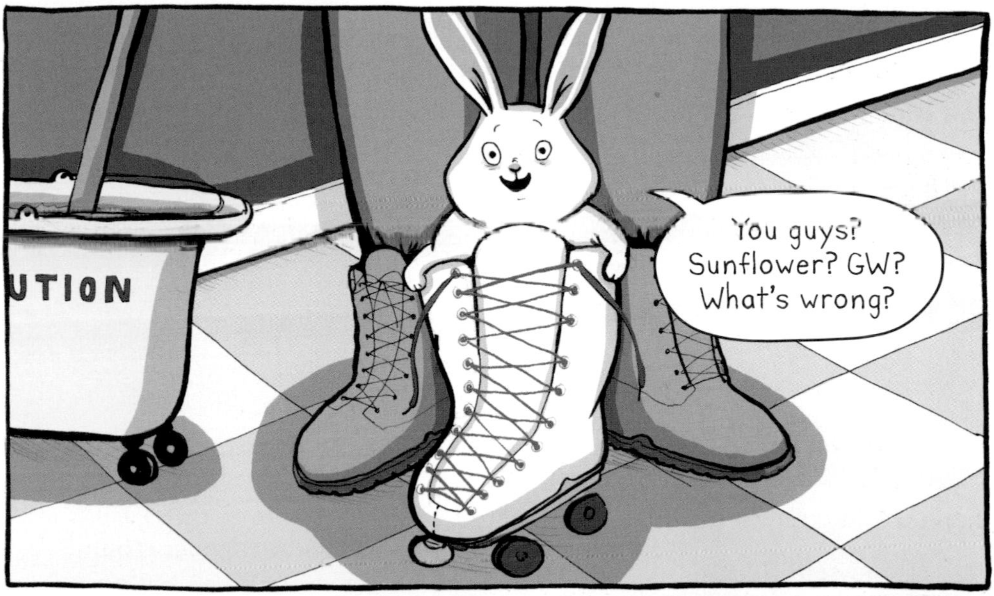
UTION
You guys?
Sunflower? GW?
What's wrong?

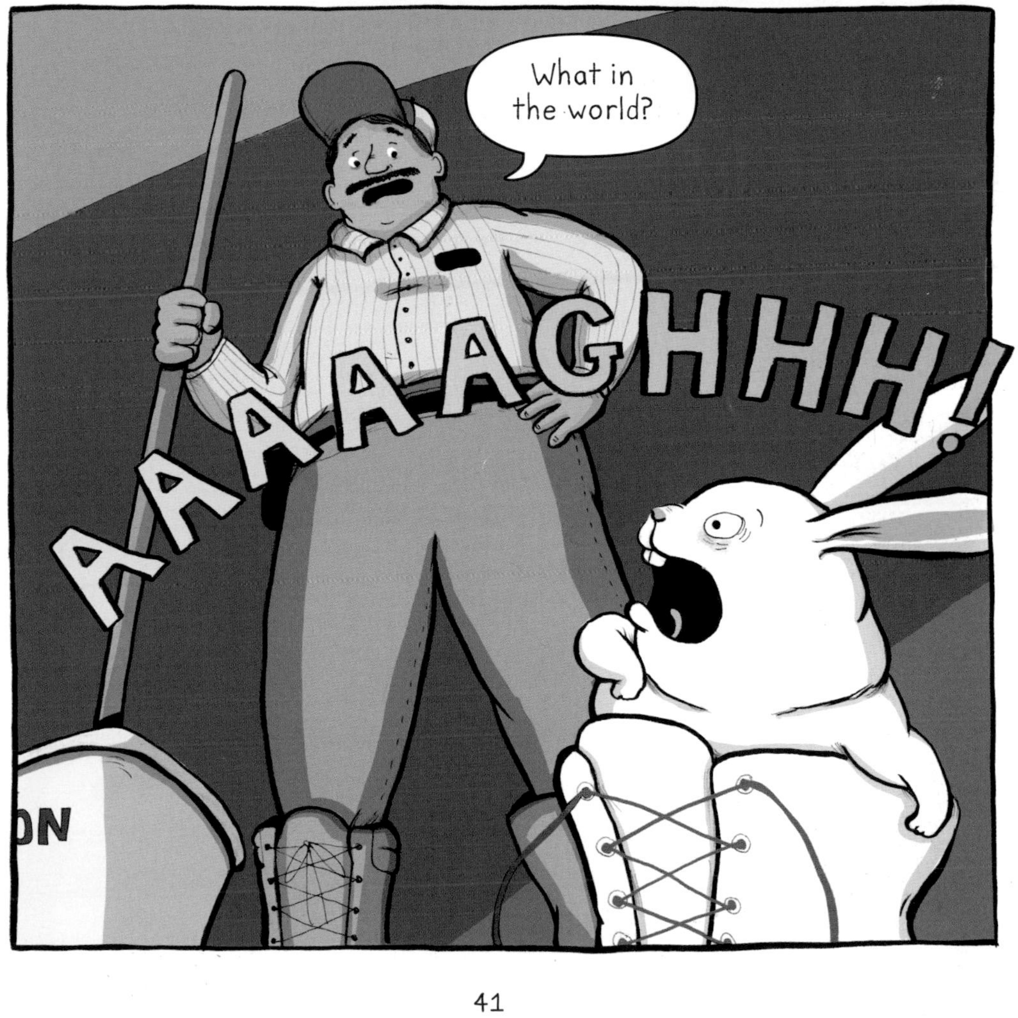
What in
the world?
AAAAAGHHH!
ON

Don't you belong in the first-grade classroom?

Quick, GW! Park the cars here. You get Barry—I'll take care of Mr. Martin.

What? There are MORE of you?!?

GW, help!

Come on! I don't think we want to be around for Sunflower's plan....

Arrrrgh! The laces are stuck!

Hey, you! Stop that!

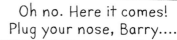

CAUTION

Oh no. Here it comes! Plug your nose, Barry....

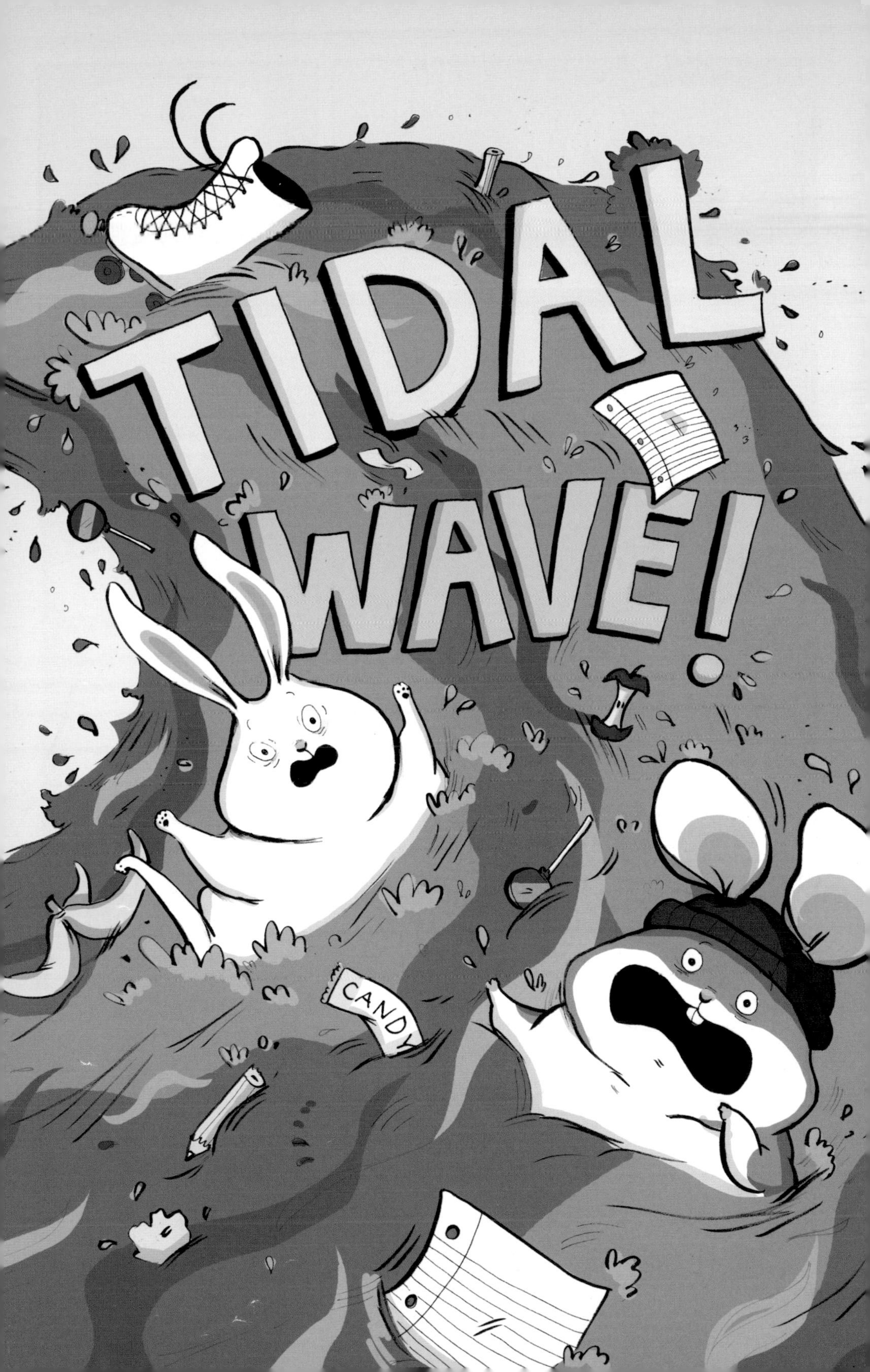
TIDAL WAVE!
CANDY

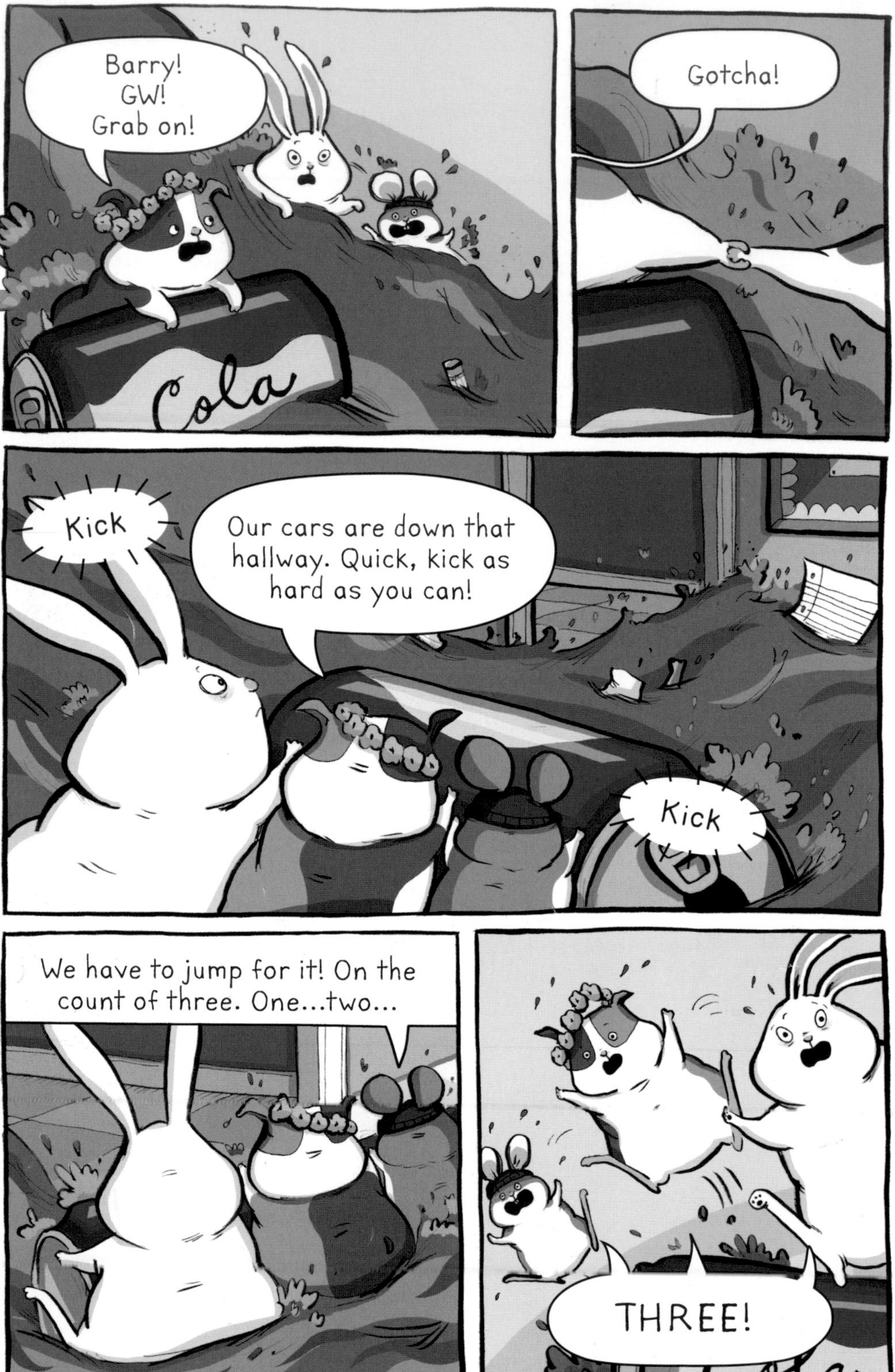
Barry!
GW!
Grab on!
Gotcha!
Kick
Our cars are down that hallway. Quick, kick as hard as you can!
Kick
We have to jump for it! On the count of three. One...two...
THREE!
Cola

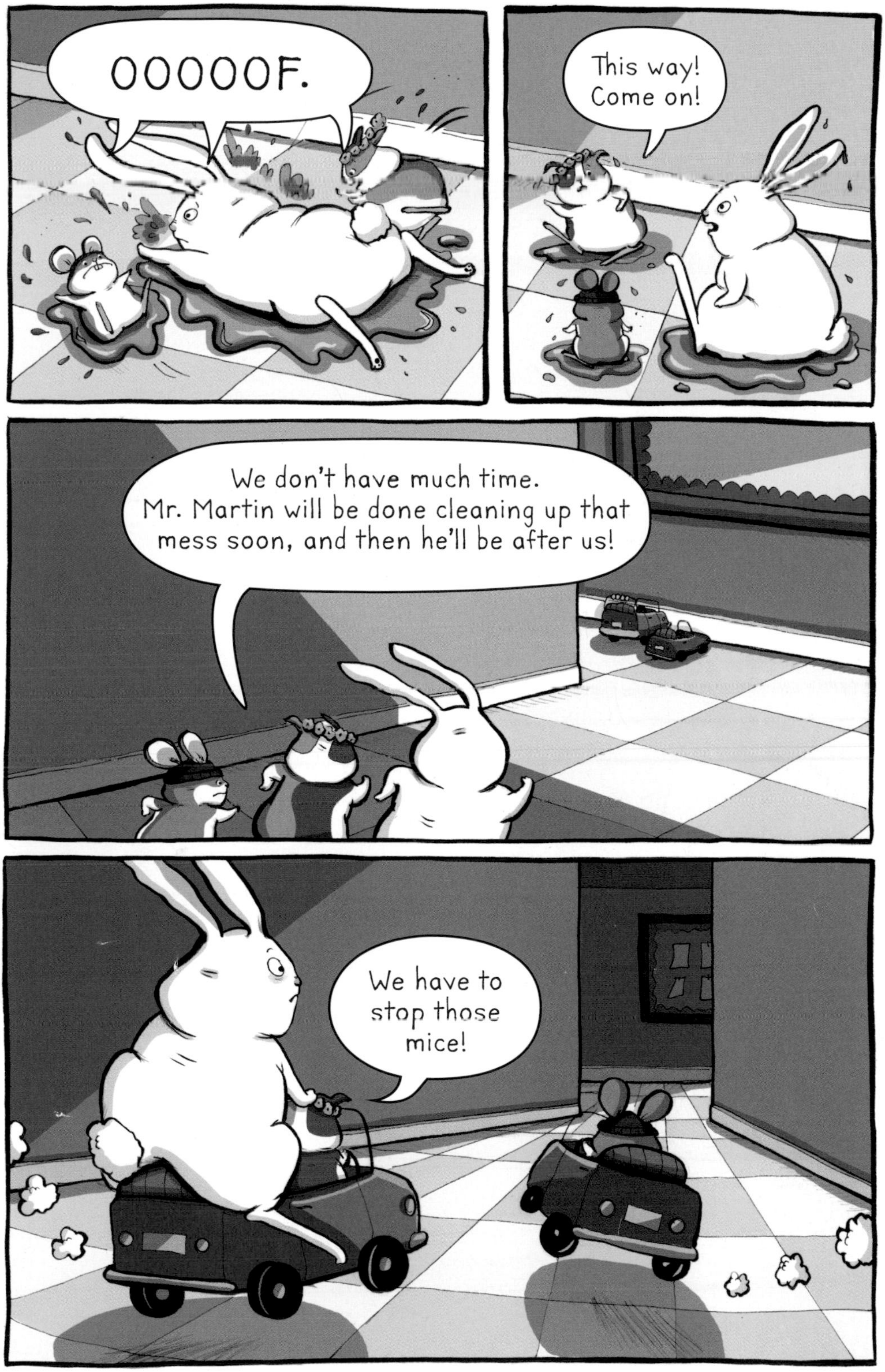
OOOOOF.
This way! Come on!
We don't have much time. Mr. Martin will be done cleaning up that mess soon, and then he'll be after us!
We have to stop those mice!

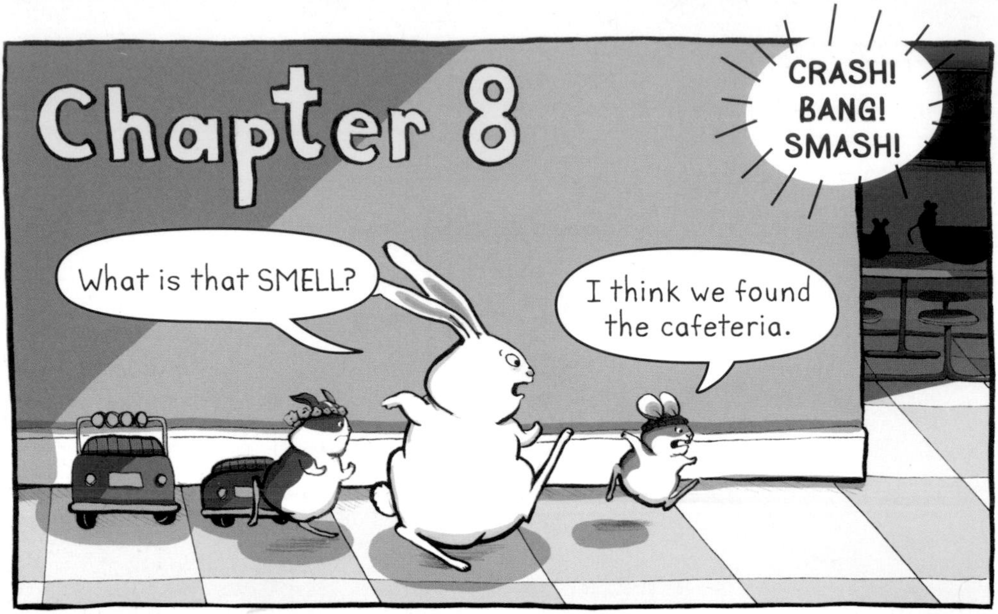
Chapter 8
CRASH! BANG! SMASH!
What is that SMELL?
I think we found the cafeteria.

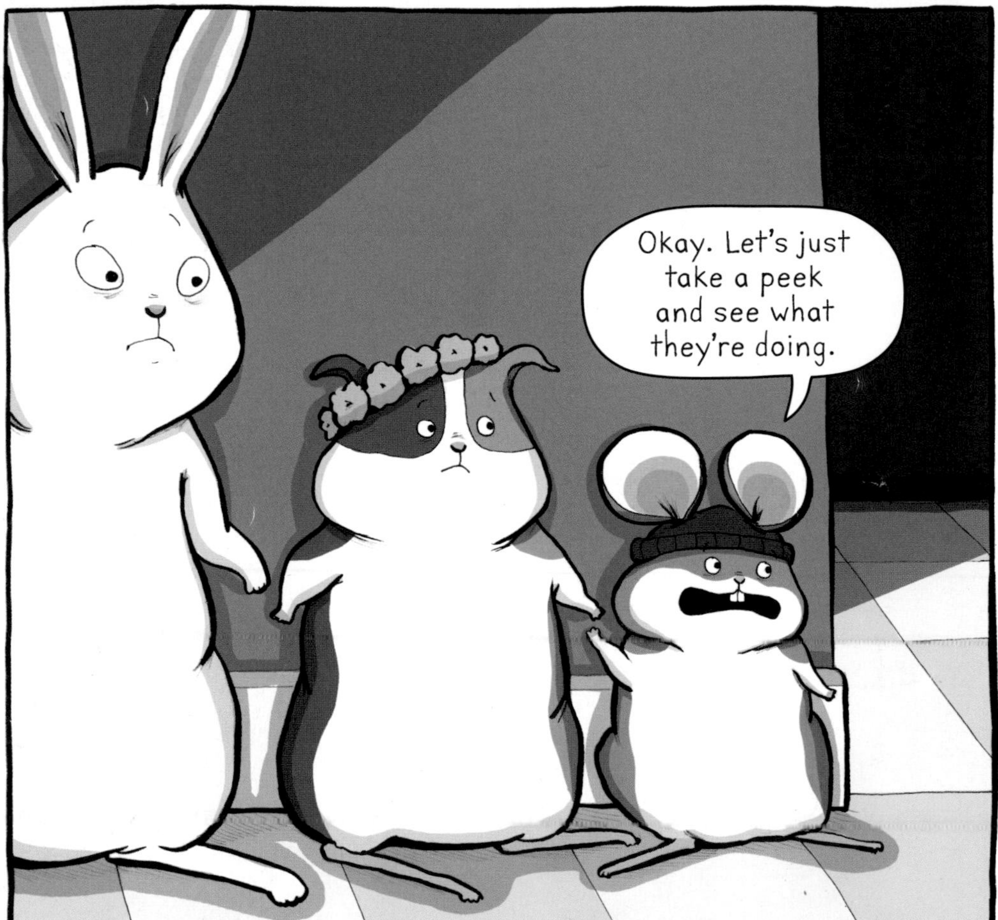
Okay. Let's just take a peek and see what they're doing.

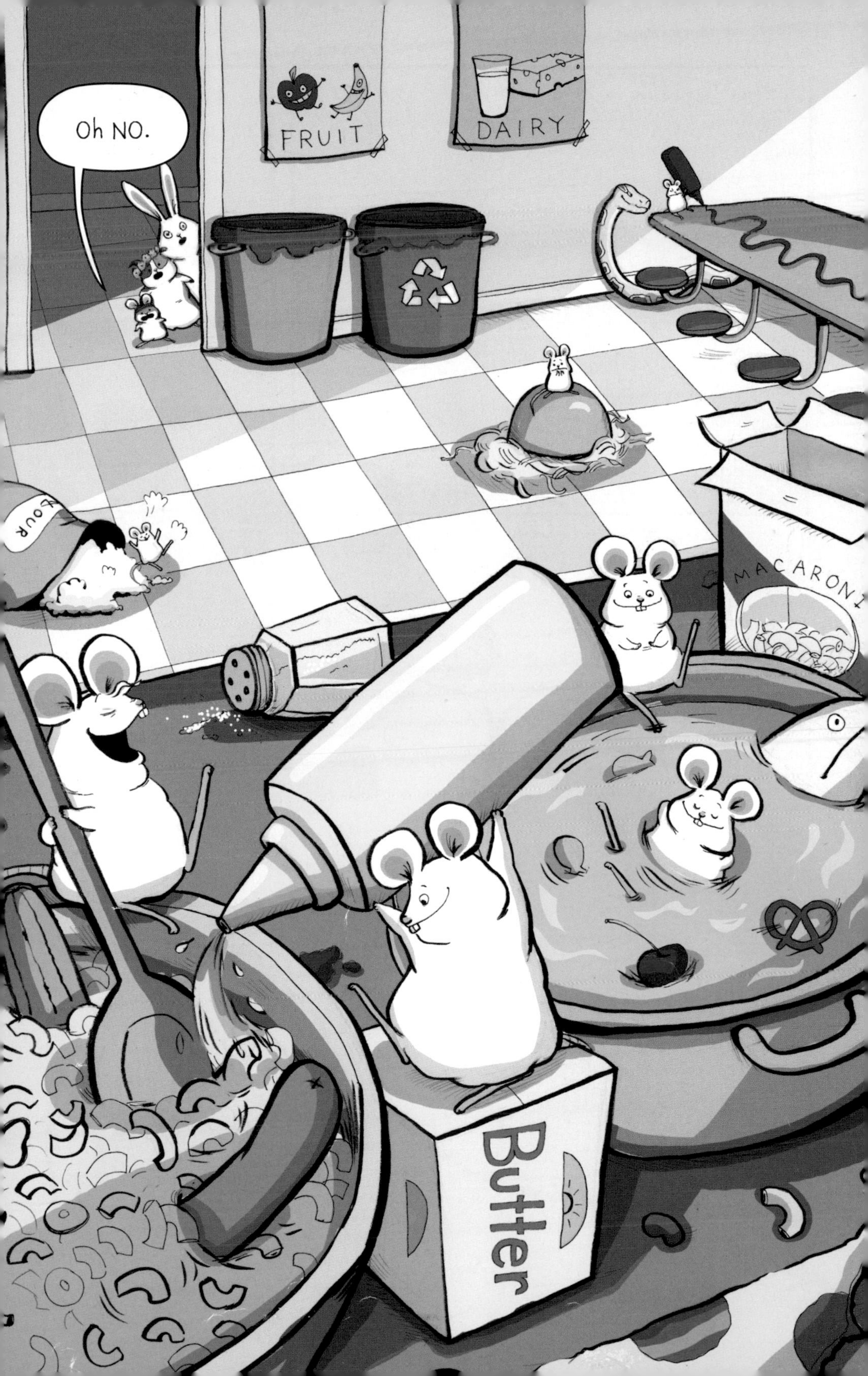
Oh NO.
FRUIT
DAIRY
MACARONI
Butter

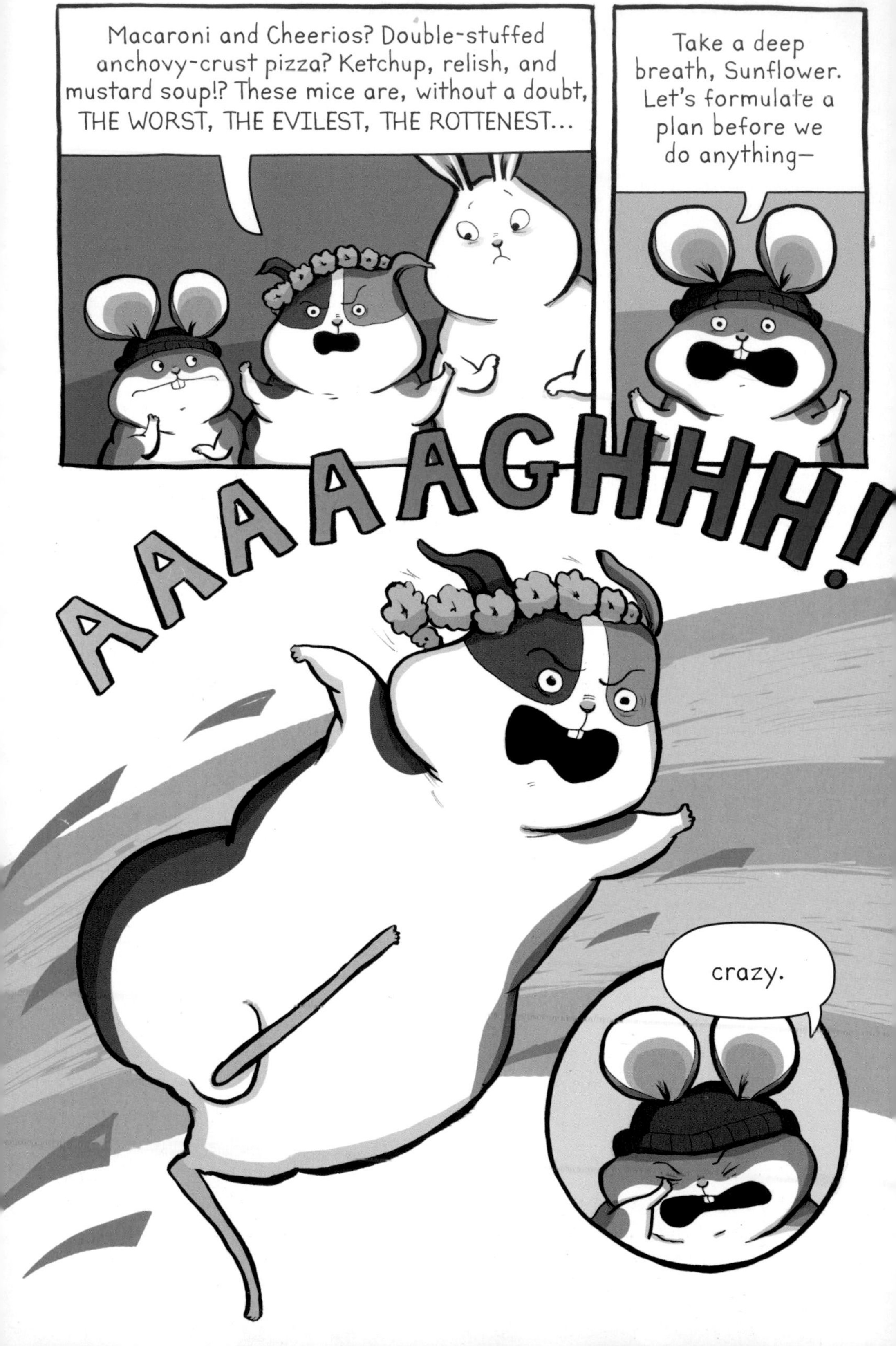
Macaroni and Cheerios? Double-stuffed anchovy-crust pizza? Ketchup, relish, and mustard soup!? These mice are, without a doubt, THE WORST, THE EVILEST, THE ROTTENEST...
Take a deep breath, Sunflower. Let's formulate a plan before we do anything—
AAAAAAGHHHH!
crazy.

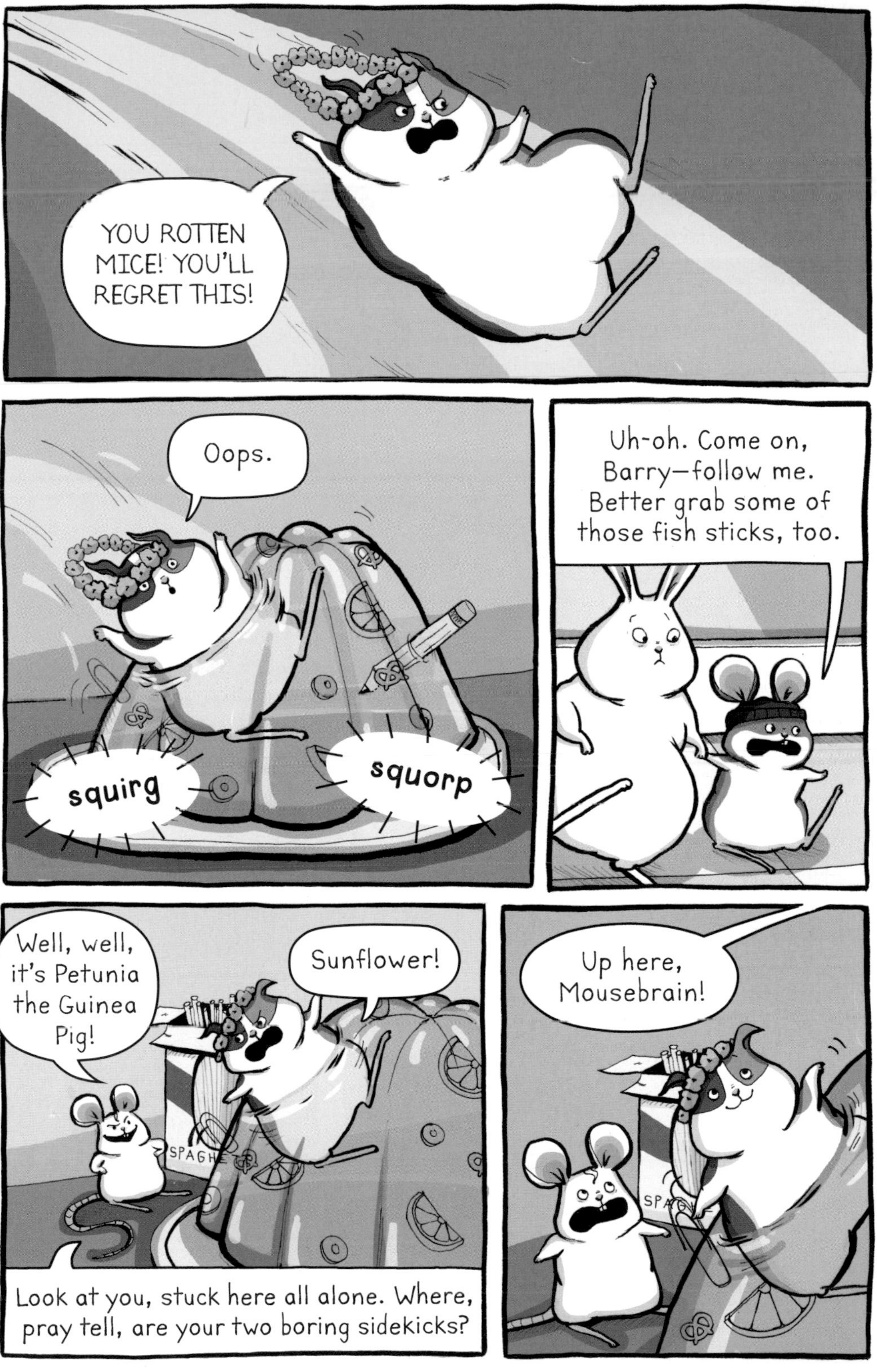

YOU ROTTEN MICE! YOU'LL REGRET THIS!
Oops.
squirg
squorp
Uh-oh. Come on, Barry—follow me. Better grab some of those fish sticks, too.
Well, well, it's Petunia the Guinea Pig!
Sunflower!
SPAGHE
Look at you, stuck here all alone. Where, pray tell, are your two boring sidekicks?
Up here, Mousebrain!

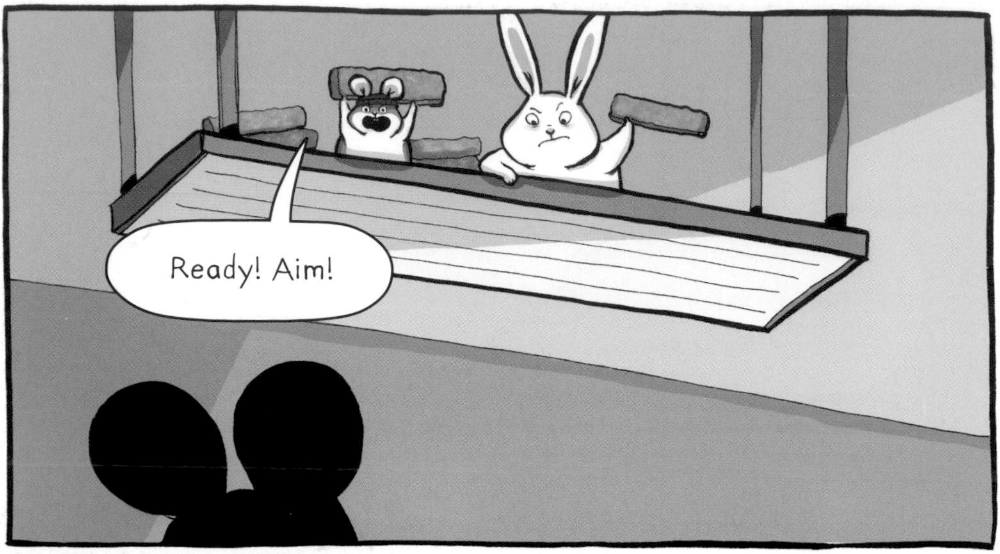
Ready! Aim!

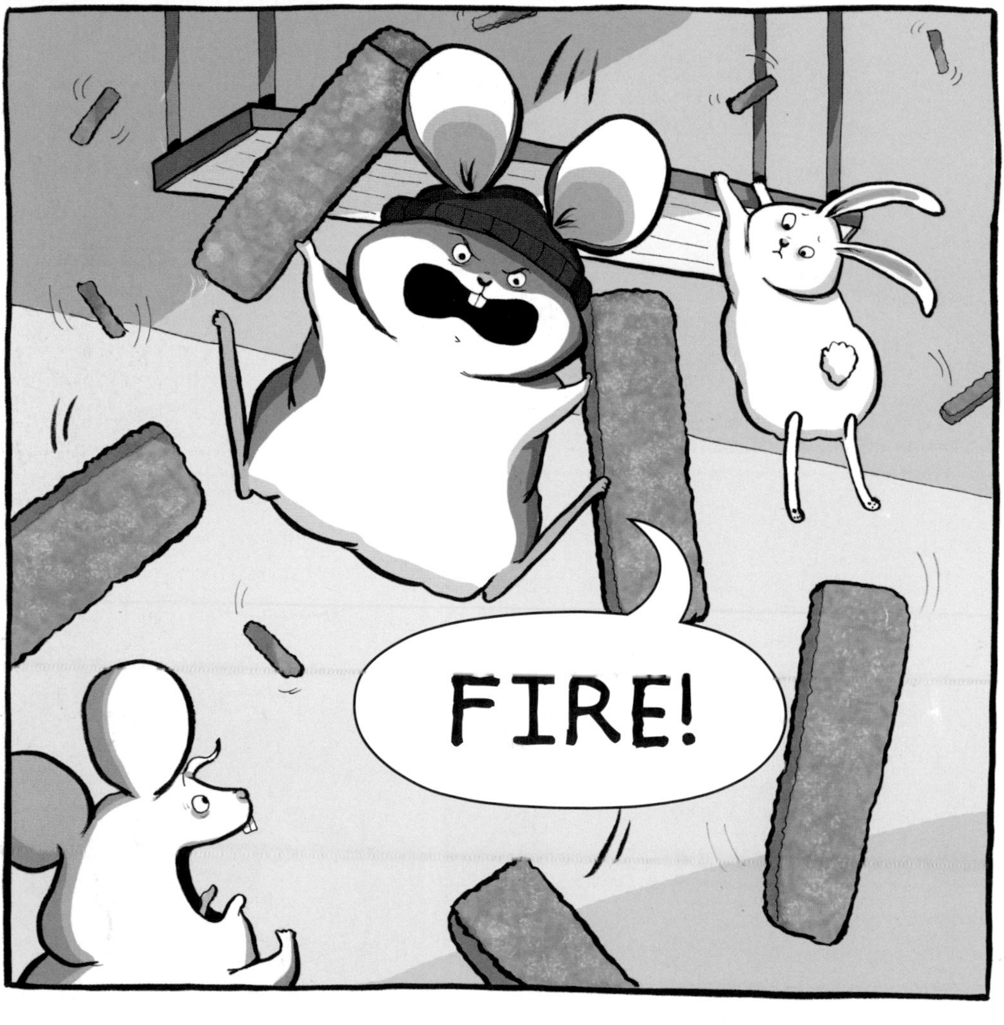
FIRE!

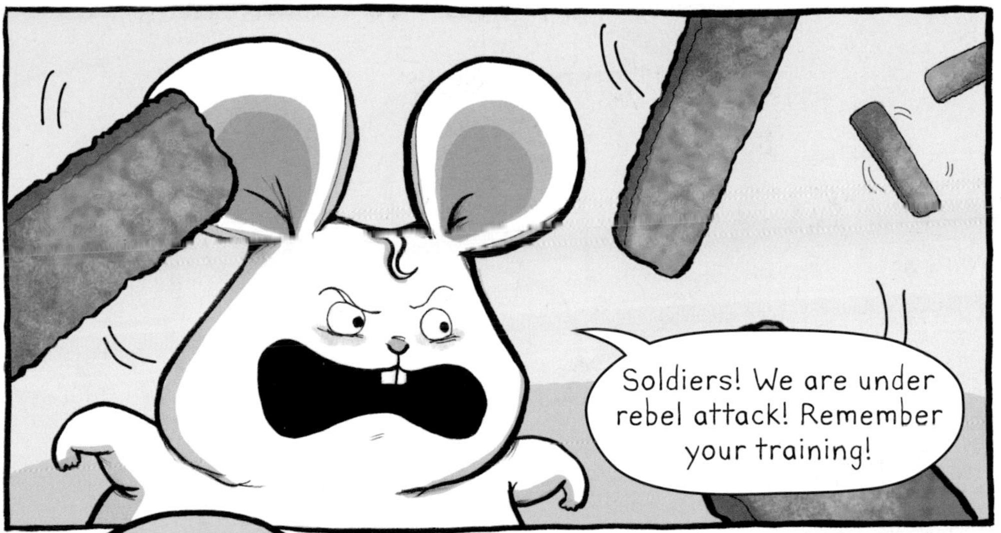
Soldiers! We are under rebel attack! Remember your training!

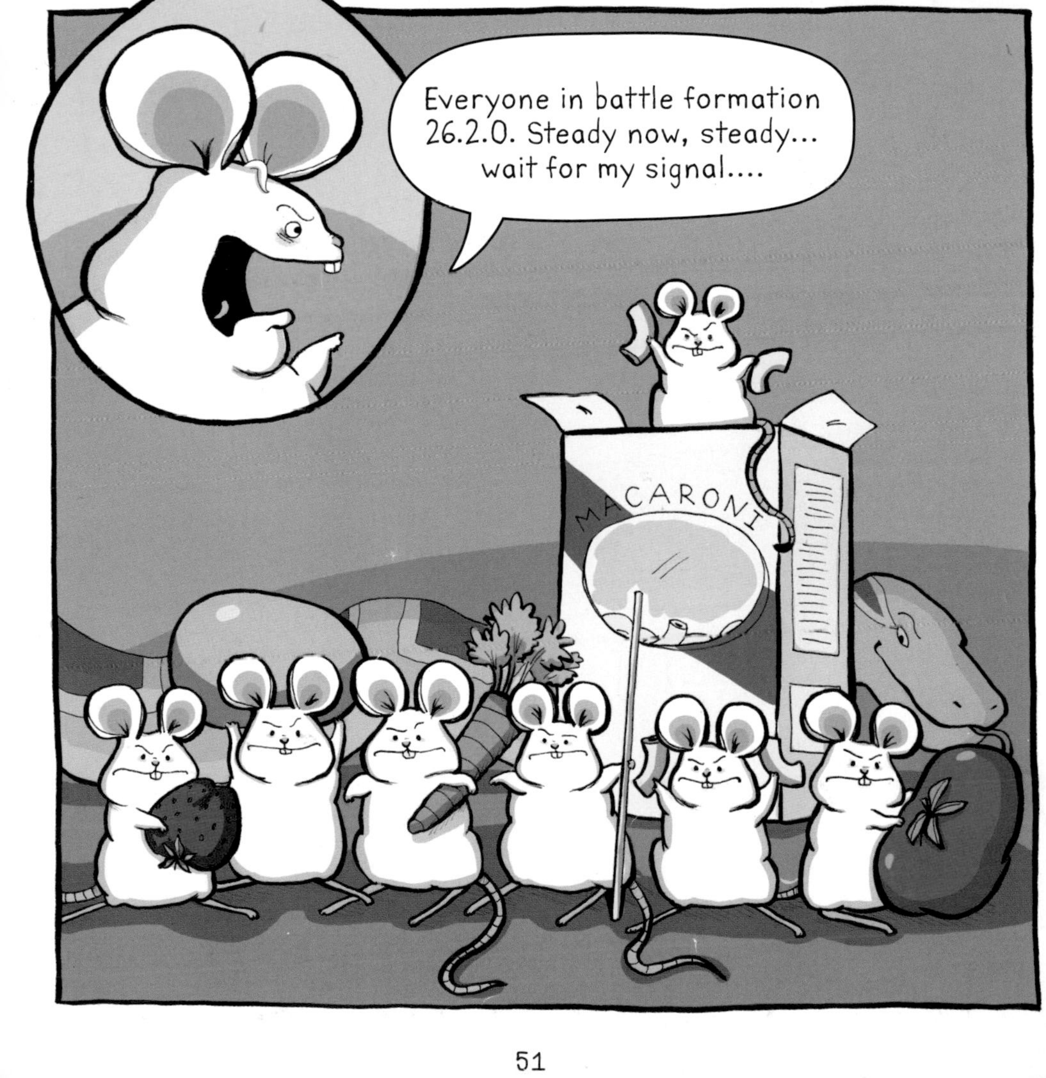
Everyone in battle formation 26.2.0. Steady now, steady... wait for my signal....
MACARONI

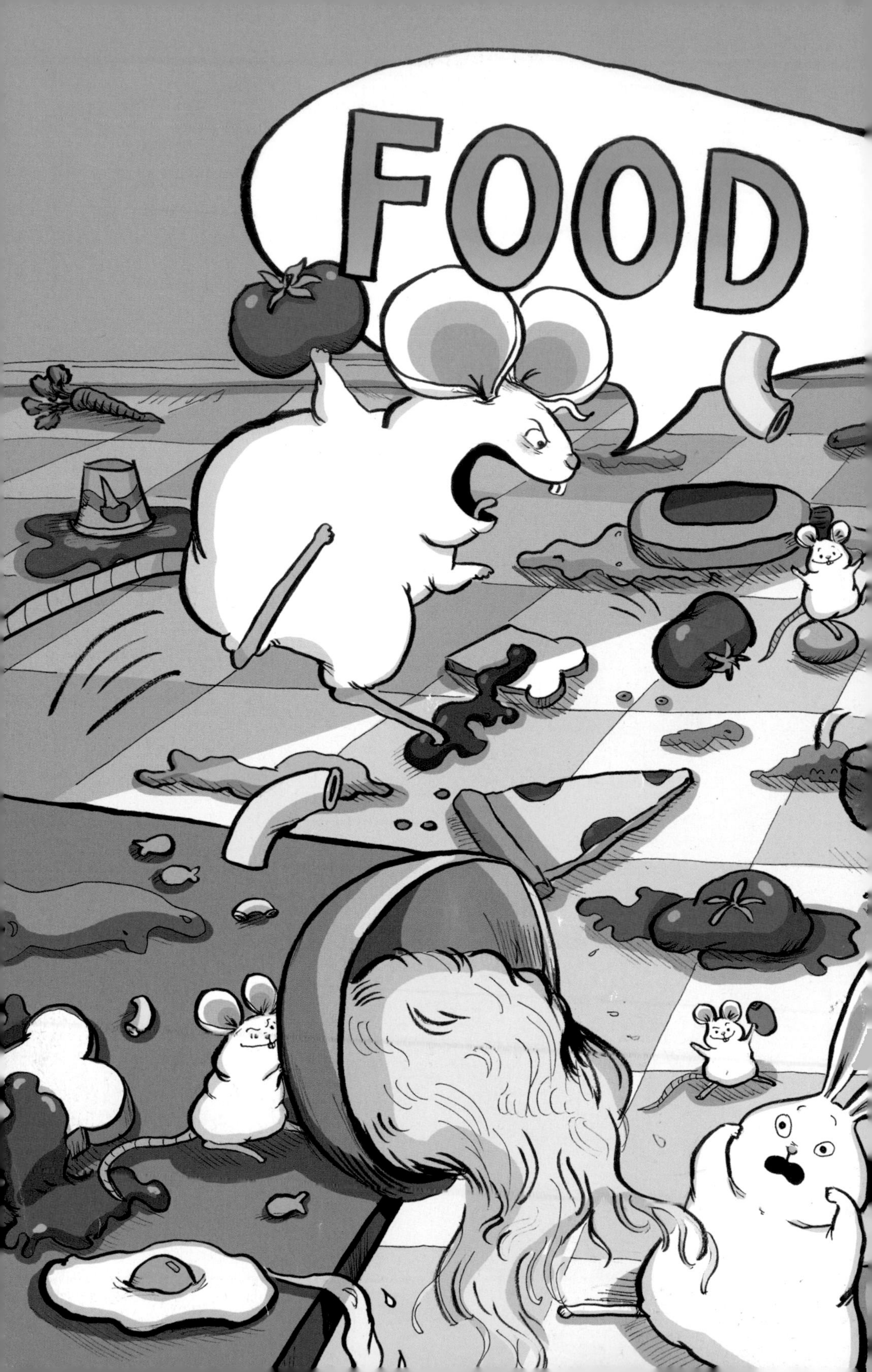
FOOD

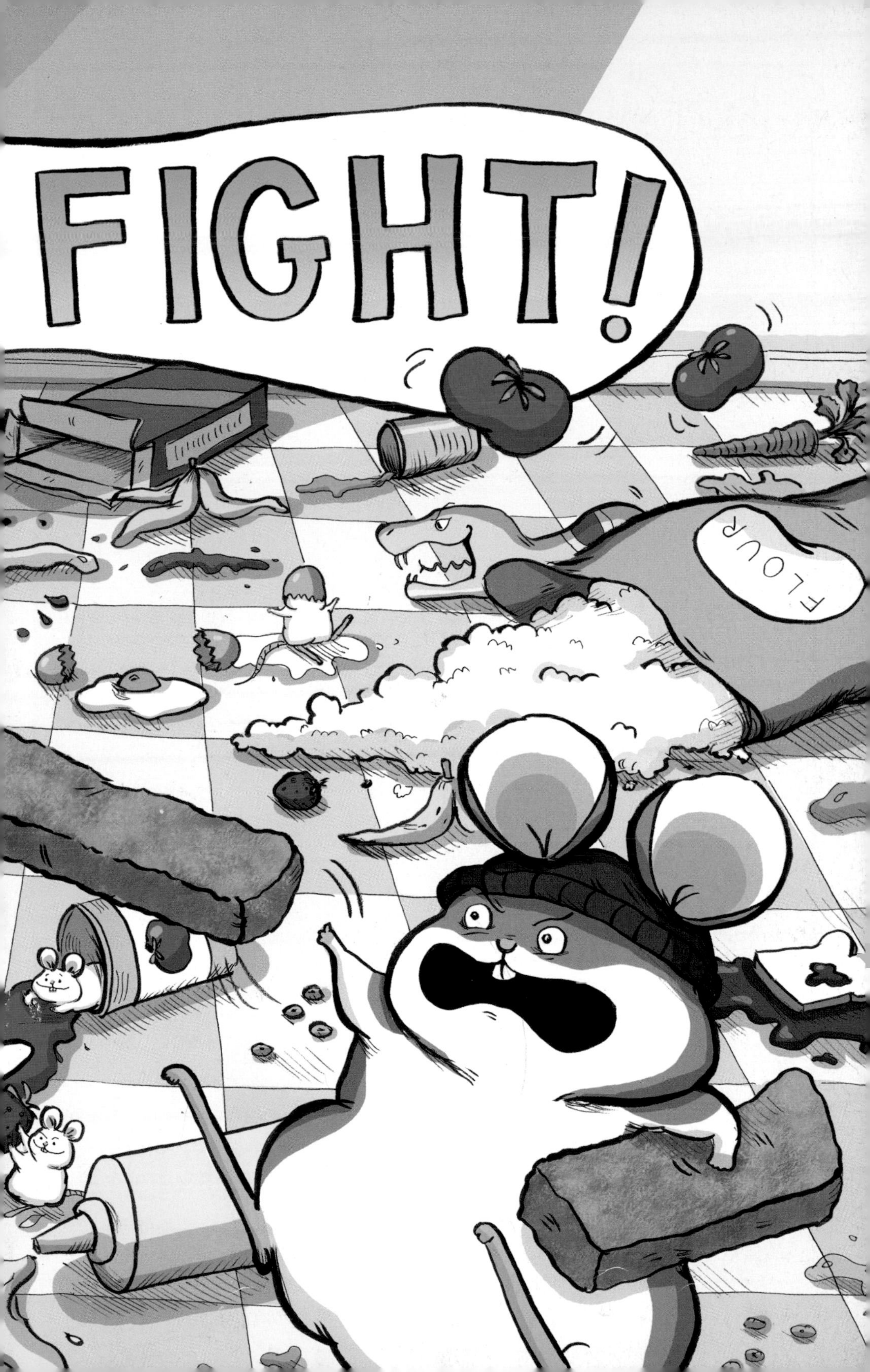
FIGHT!
FLOUR

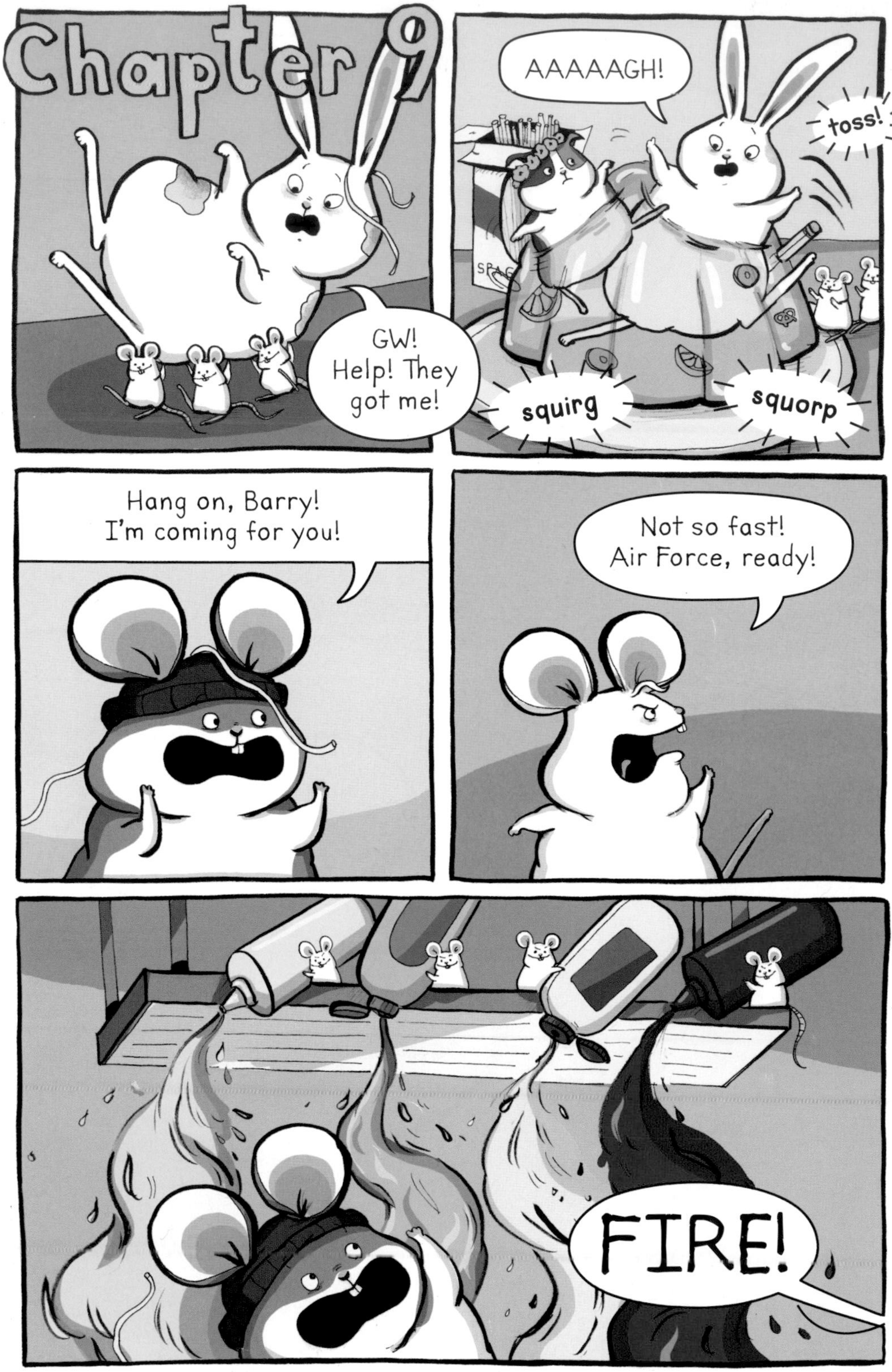
Chapter 9
GW! Help! They got me!
AAAAAGH!
toss!
squirg
squorp
Hang on, Barry! I'm coming for you!
Not so fast! Air Force, ready!
FIRE!

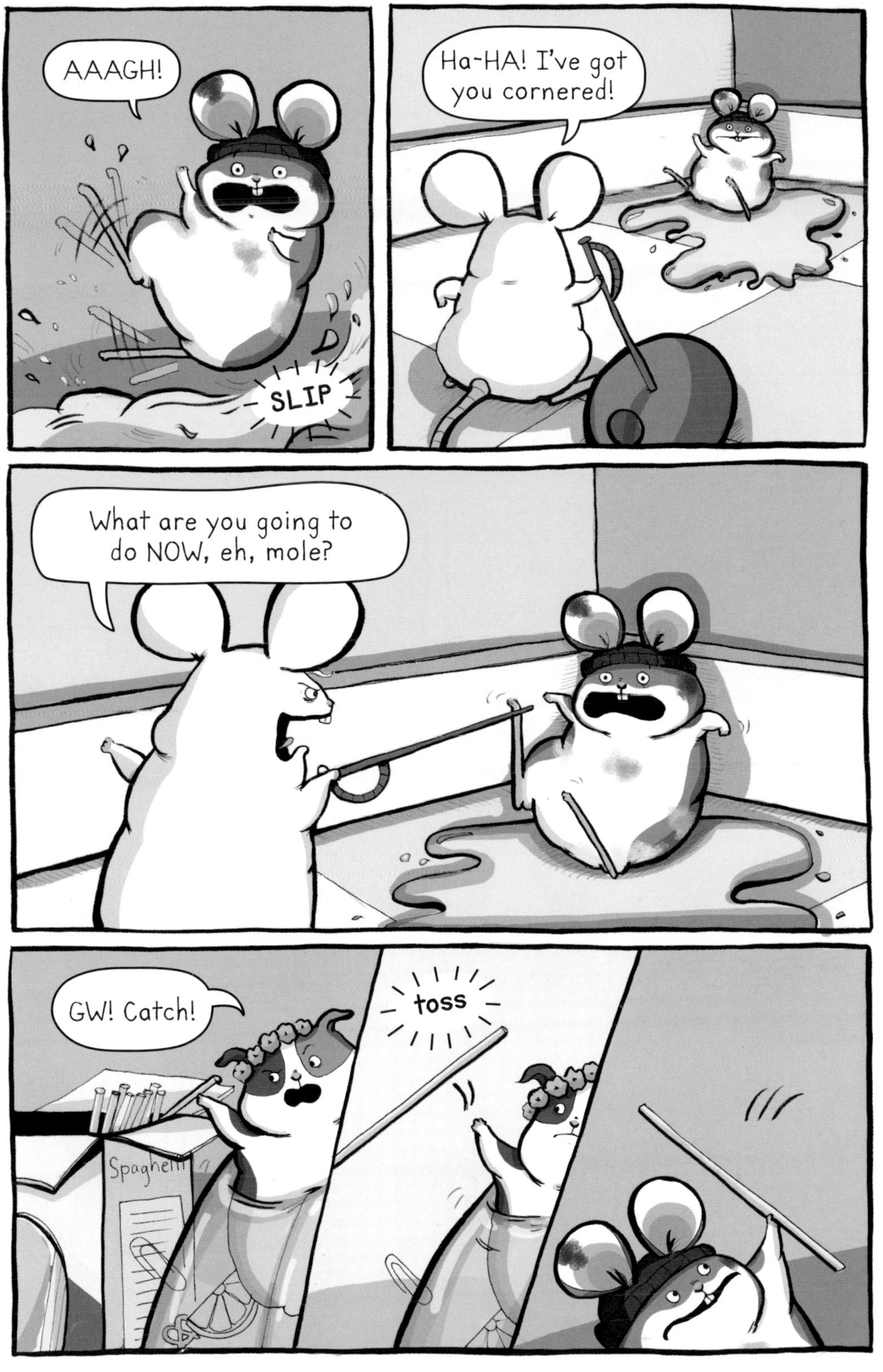
AAAGH!
SLIP
Ha-HA! I've got you cornered!
What are you going to do NOW, eh, mole?
GW! Catch!
toss
Spaghetti

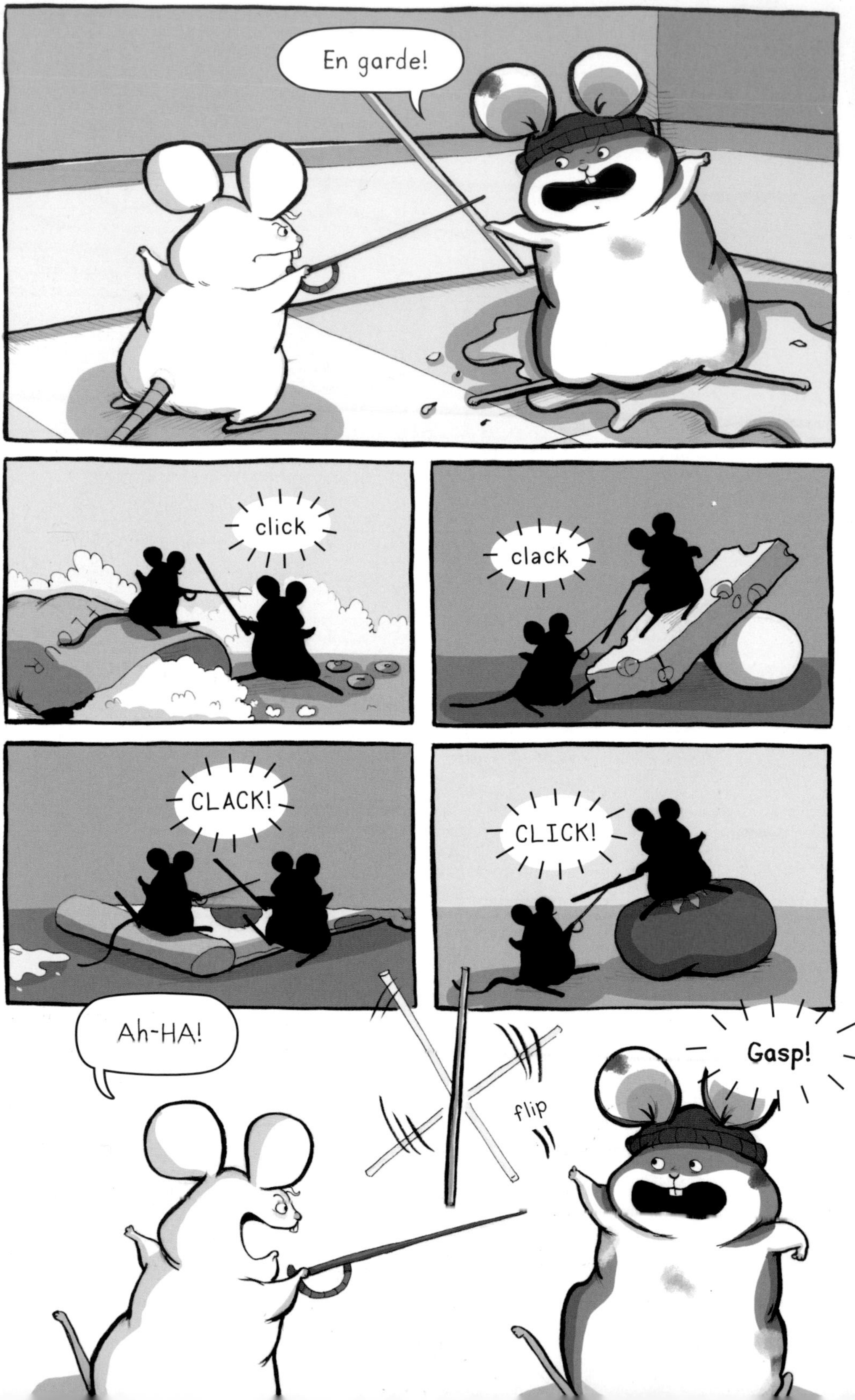
En garde!
click
clack
CLACK!
CLICK!
Ah-HA!
flip
Gasp!

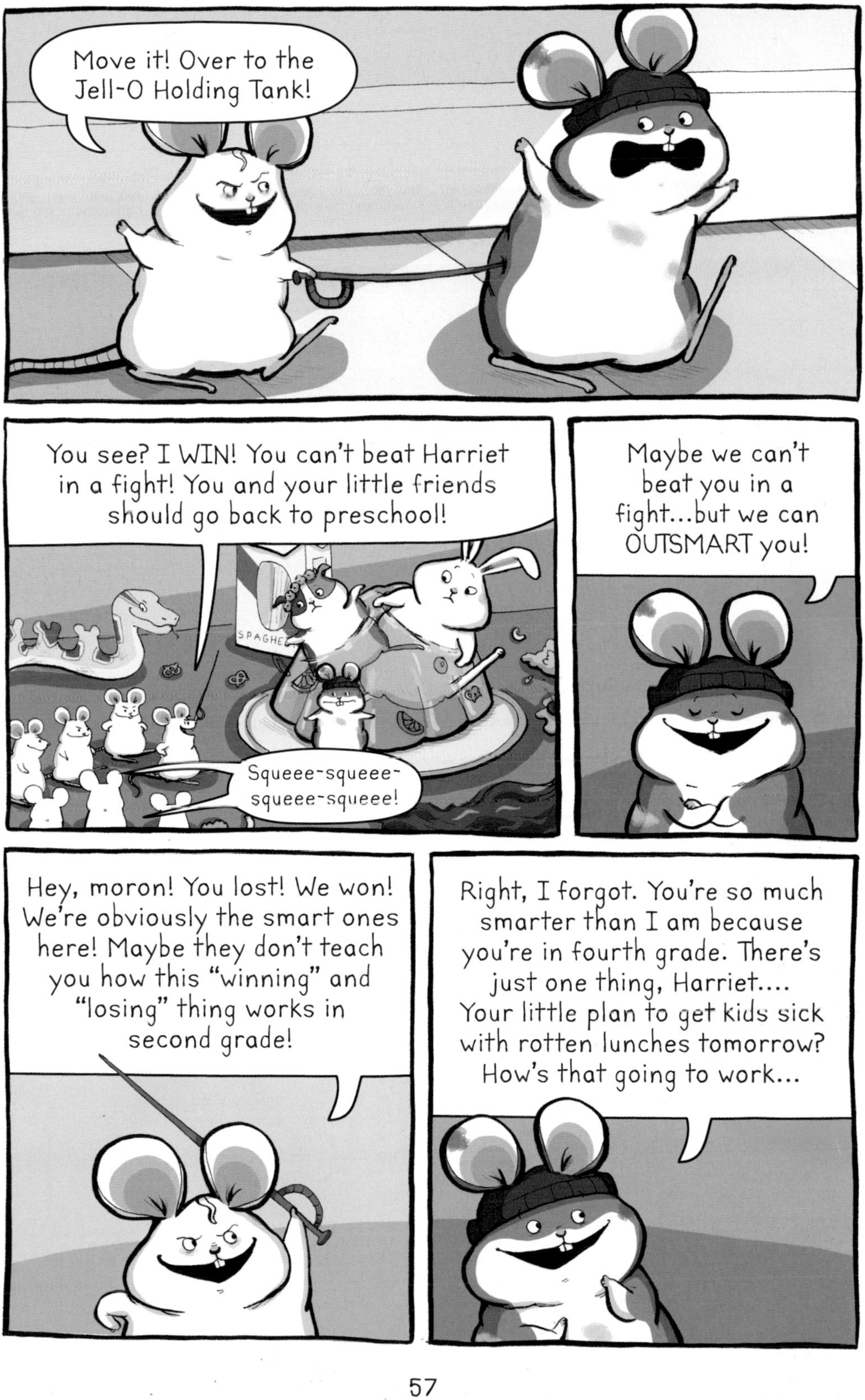

Move it! Over to the Jell-O Holding Tank!
You see? I WIN! You can't beat Harriet in a fight! You and your little friends should go back to preschool!
SPAGHE
Squeee-squeee-squeee-squeee!
Maybe we can't beat you in a fight...but we can OUTSMART you!
Hey, moron! You lost! We won! We're obviously the smart ones here! Maybe they don't teach you how this "winning" and "losing" thing works in second grade!
Right, I forgot. You're so much smarter than I am because you're in fourth grade. There's just one thing, Harriet.... Your little plan to get kids sick with rotten lunches tomorrow? How's that going to work...

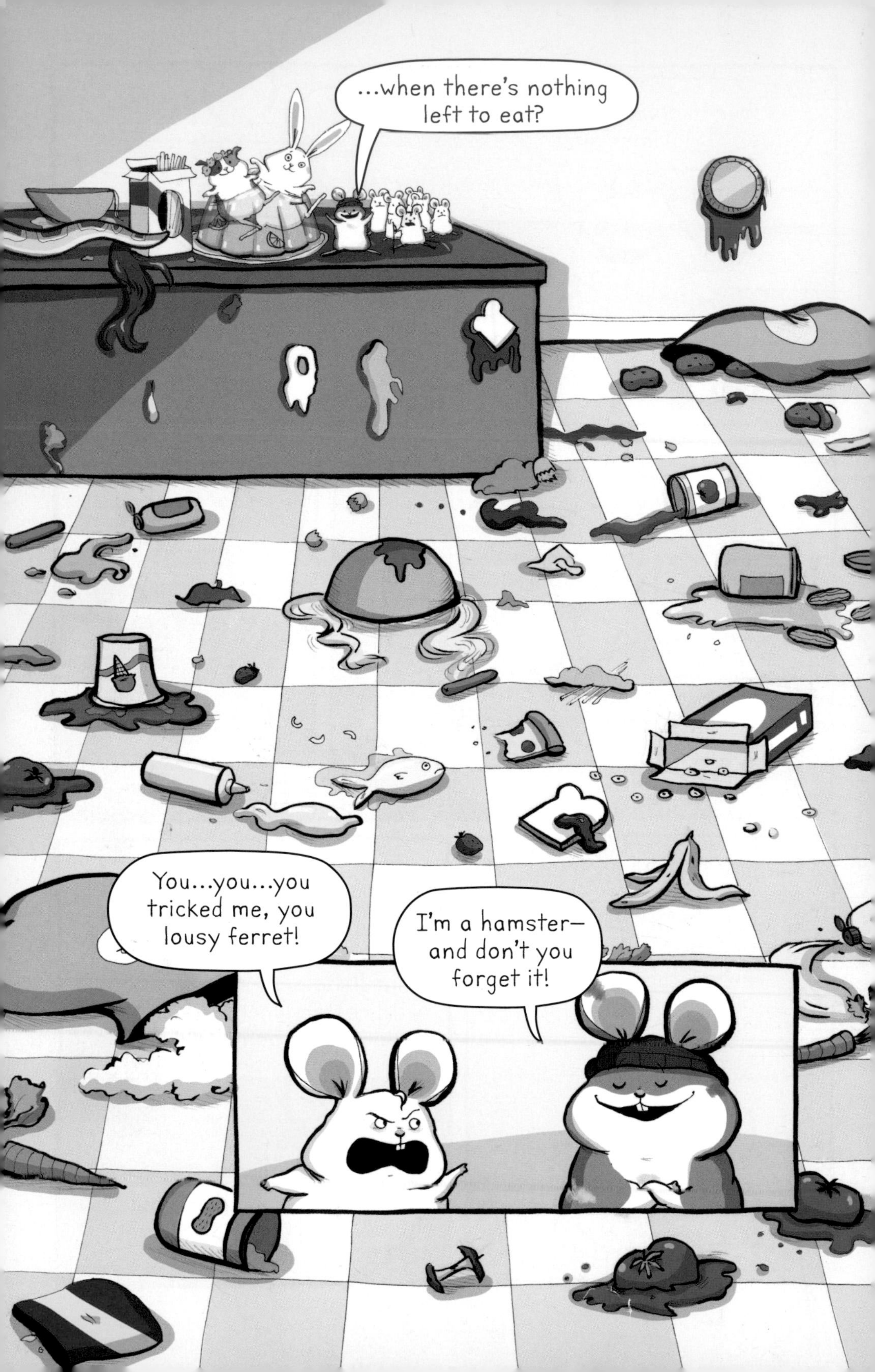
...when there's nothing left to eat?
You...you...you tricked me, you lousy ferret!
I'm a hamster—and don't you forget it!

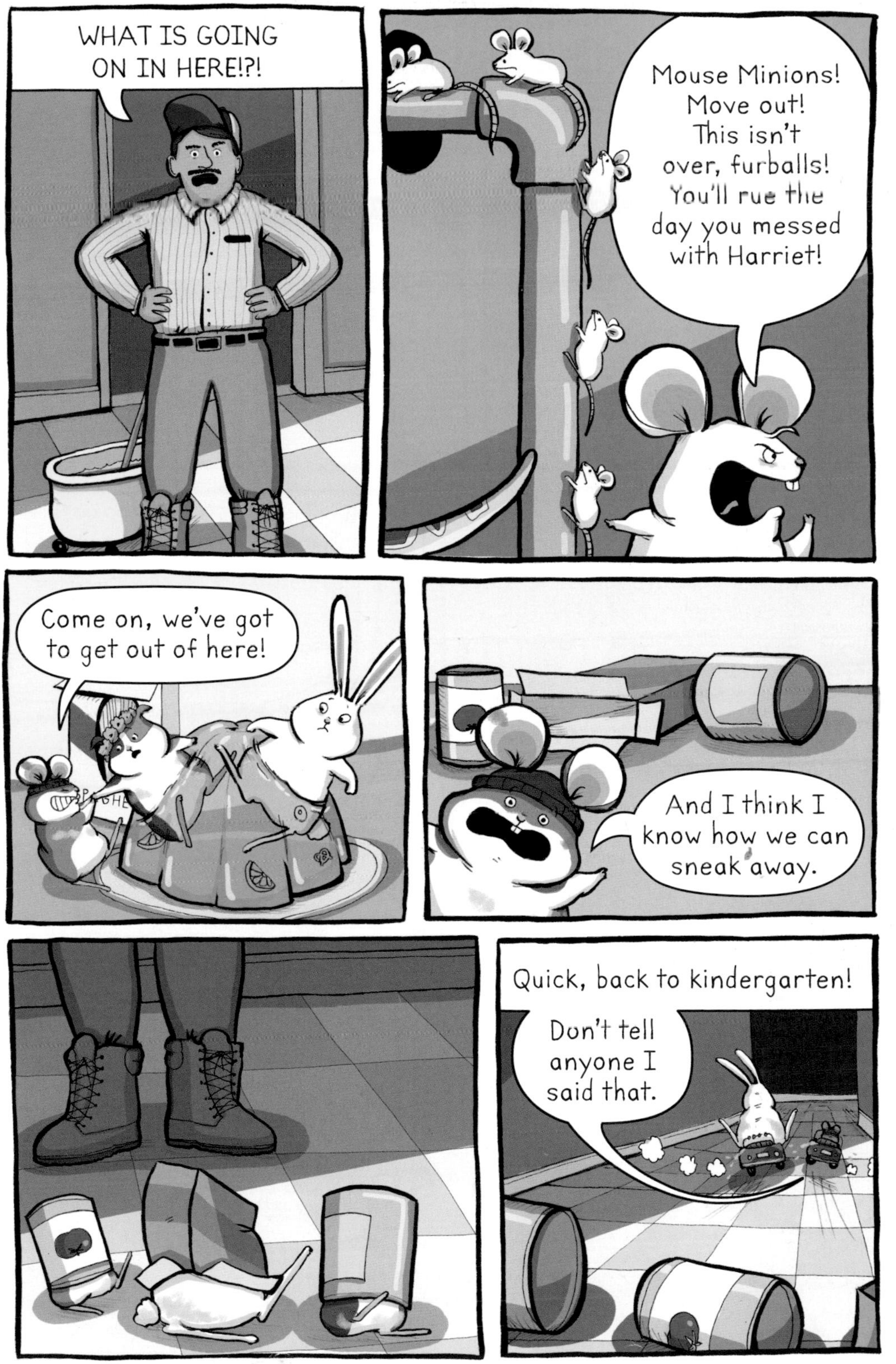
WHAT IS GOING ON IN HERE!?!
Mouse Minions! Move out! This isn't over, furballs! You'll rue the day you messed with Harriet!
Come on, we've got to get out of here!
And I think I know how we can sneak away.
Quick, back to kindergarten!
Don't tell anyone I said that.

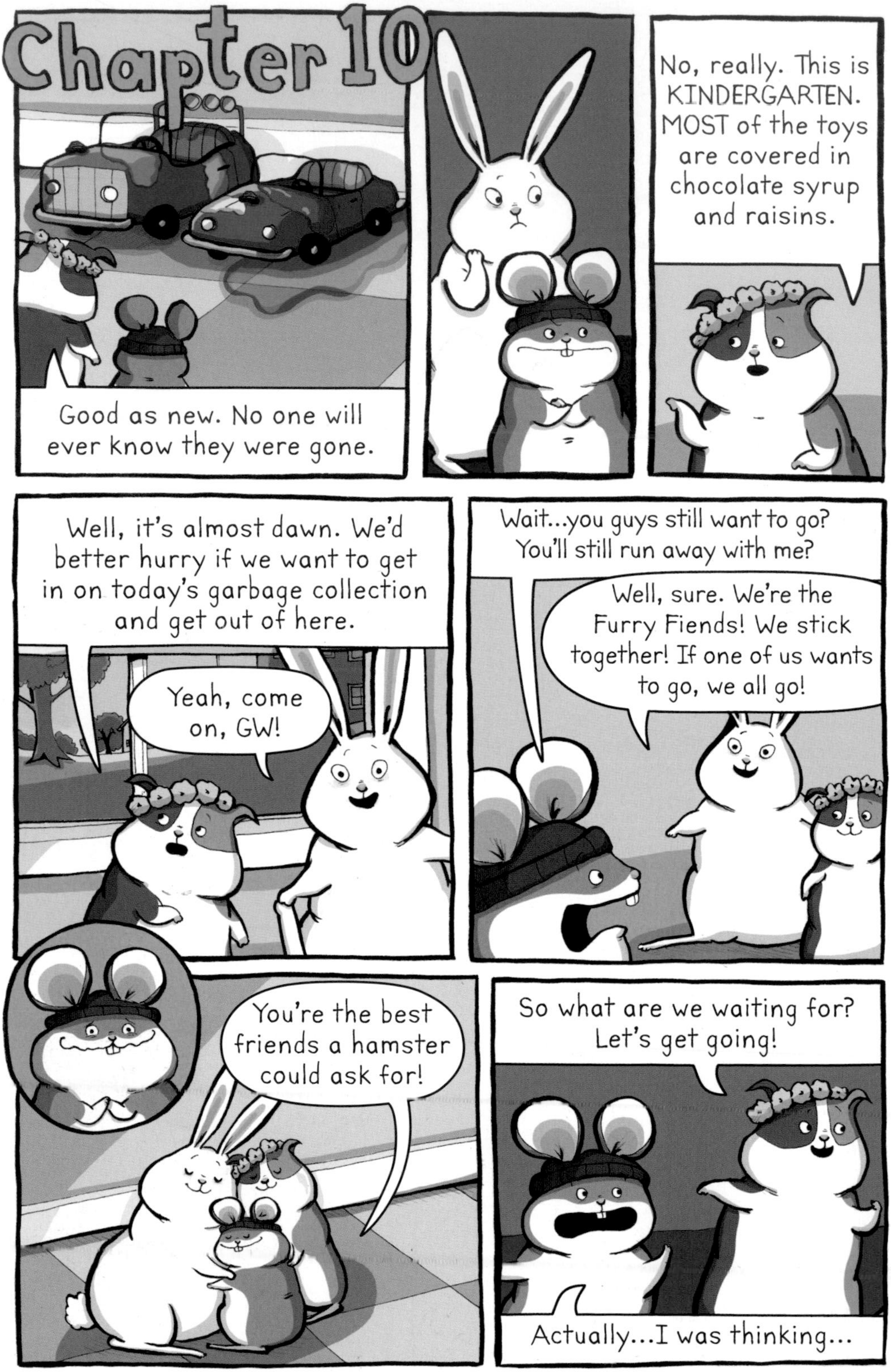
Chapter 10
Good as new. No one will ever know they were gone.
No, really. This is KINDERGARTEN. MOST of the toys are covered in chocolate syrup and raisins.
Well, it's almost dawn. We'd better hurry if we want to get in on today's garbage collection and get out of here.
Yeah, come on, GW!
Wait...you guys still want to go? You'll still run away with me?
Well, sure. We're the Furry Fiends! We stick together! If one of us wants to go, we all go!
You're the best friends a hamster could ask for!
So what are we waiting for? Let's get going!
Actually...I was thinking...

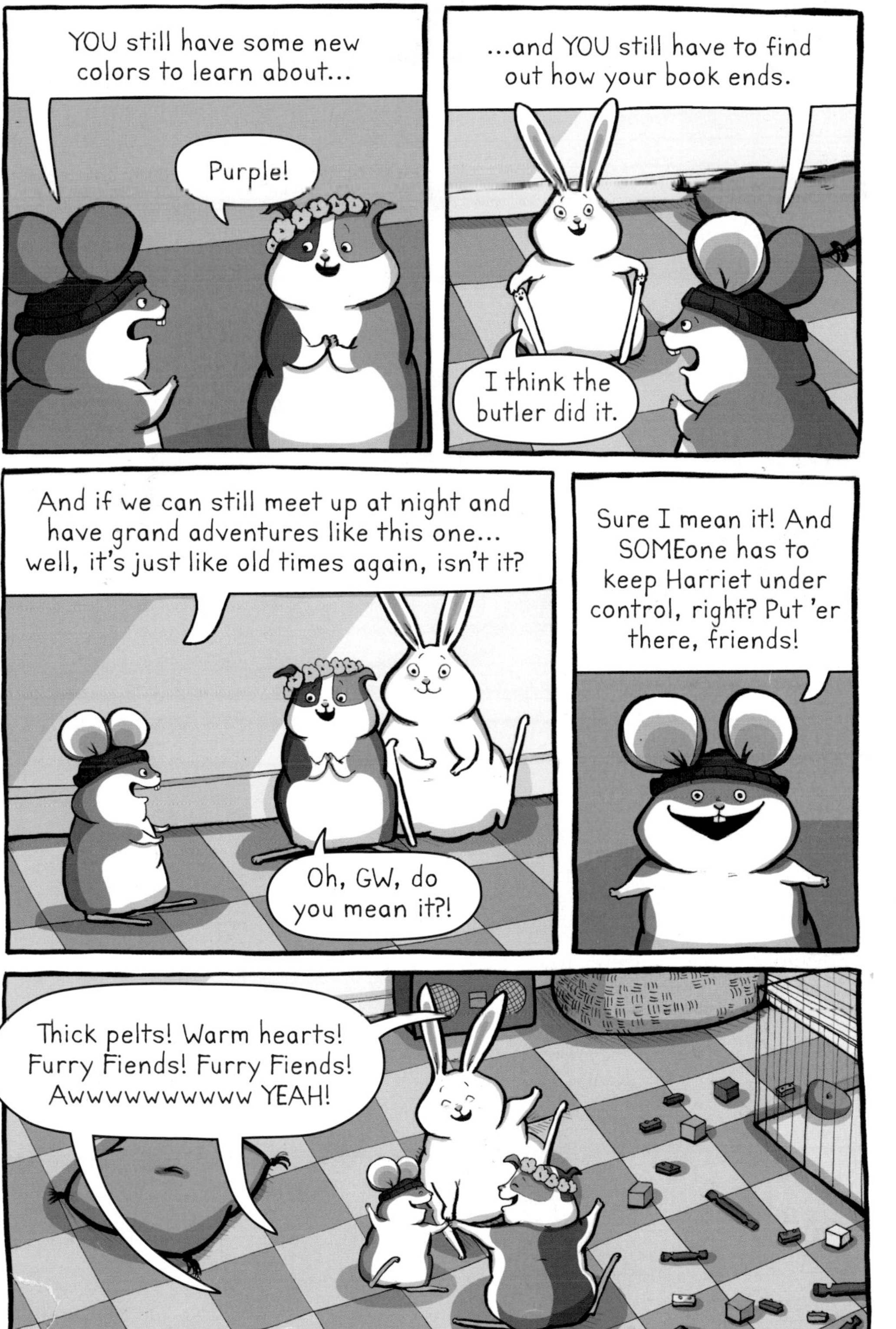
YOU still have some new colors to learn about...
Purple!
...and YOU still have to find out how your book ends.
I think the butler did it.
And if we can still meet up at night and have grand adventures like this one... well, it's just like old times again, isn't it?
Oh, GW, do you mean it?!
Sure I mean it! And SOMEone has to keep Harriet under control, right? Put 'er there, friends!
Thick pelts! Warm hearts! Furry Fiends! Furry Fiends! Awwwwwwwwww YEAH!

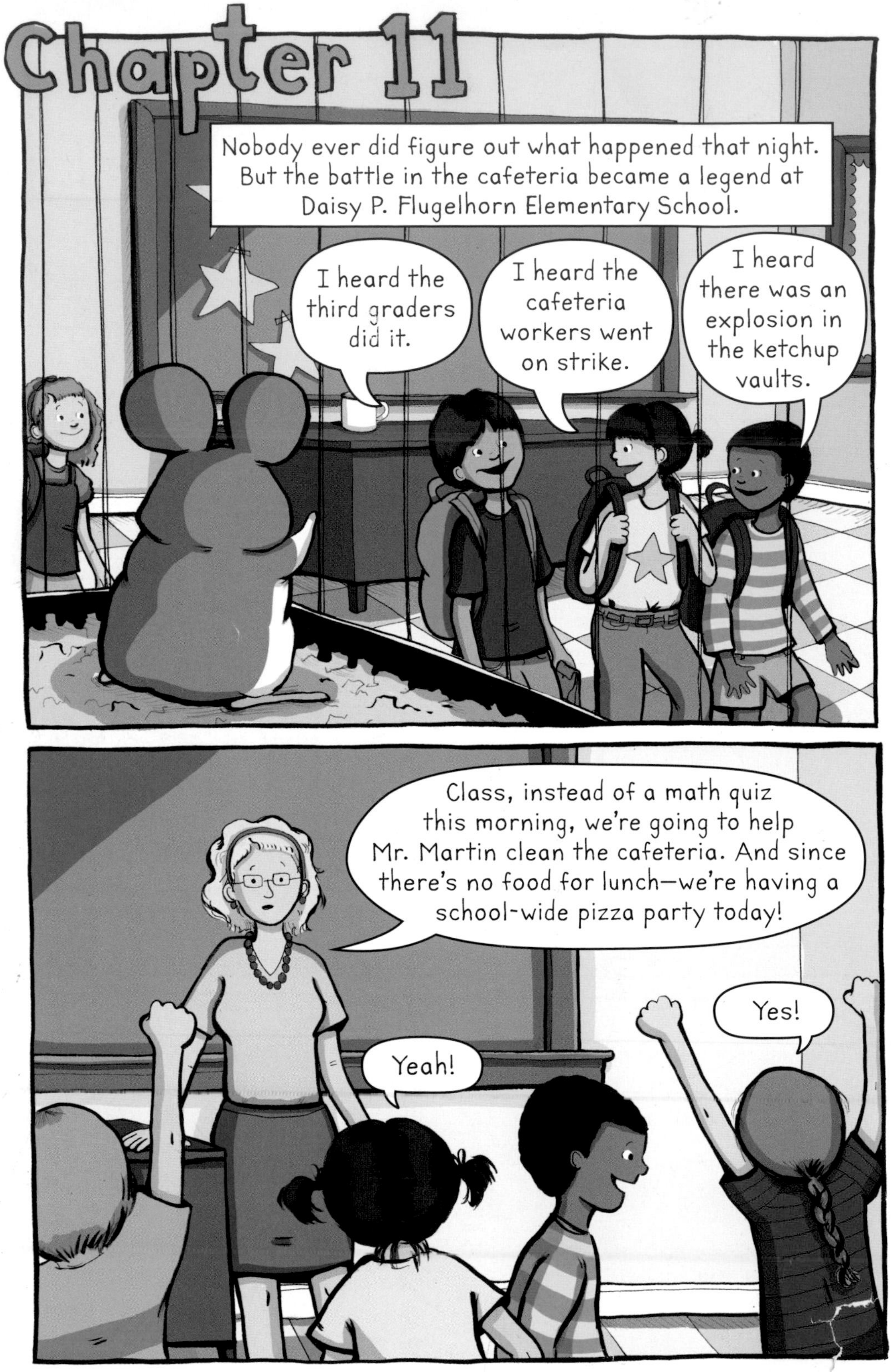
Chapter 11
Nobody ever did figure out what happened that night. But the battle in the cafeteria became a legend at Daisy P. Flugelhorn Elementary School.
I heard the third graders did it.
I heard the cafeteria workers went on strike.
I heard there was an explosion in the ketchup vaults.
Class, instead of a math quiz this morning, we're going to help Mr. Martin clean the cafeteria. And since there's no food for lunch—we're having a school-wide pizza party today!
Yeah!
Yes!

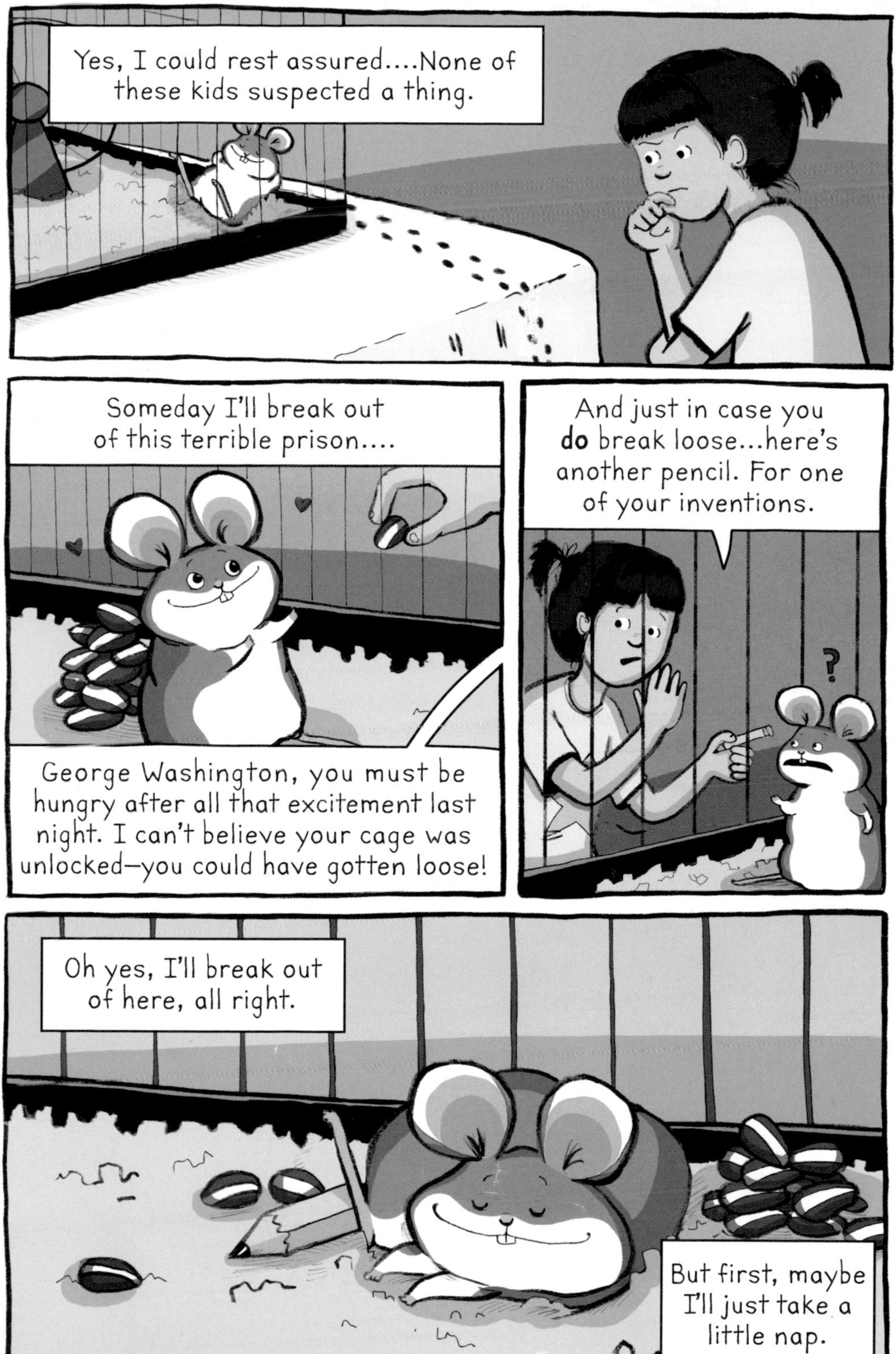
Yes, I could rest assured....None of these kids suspected a thing.
Someday I'll break out of this terrible prison....
George Washington, you must be hungry after all that excitement last night. I can't believe your cage was unlocked—you could have gotten loose!
And just in case you **do** break loose...here's another pencil. For one of your inventions.
?
Oh yes, I'll break out of here, all right.
But first, maybe I'll just take a little nap.

For Oscar, my little mouse

Henry Holt and Company, LLC
Publishers since 1866
175 Fifth Avenue
New York, New York 10010
mackids.com

Library of Congress Cataloging-in-Publication Data
Jamieson, Victoria, author, illustrator.
The great pet escape / Victoria Jamieson.—First edition.
        pages   cm
Summary: —"A young graphic novel chapter book about the escape escapades of class pets
at Daisy P. Flugelhorn Elementary School"—Provided by publisher.
ISBN 978-1-62779-105-2 (hardback)—ISBN 978-1-62779-106-9 (paperback)
1. Graphic novels. [1. Graphic novels. 2. Pets—Fiction. 3. Schools—Fiction. 4. Escapes—Fiction.
5. Humorous stories.] I. Title.
PZ7.7.J36Gr 2016   741.5'973—dc23   2015003257

ISBN (HC) 978-1-62779-105-2
1 3 5 7 9 10 8 6 4 2

ISBN (PB) 978-1-62779-106-9
1 3 5 7 9 10 8 6 4 2

Our books may be purchased in bulk for promotional, educational, or business use.
Please contact your local bookseller or the Macmillan Corporate and Premium Sales Department
at (800) 221-7945 ext. 5442 or by e-mail at MacmillanSpecialMarkets@macmillan.com.

First Edition—2016
The illustrations for this book were created with pen and ink; color was added digitally.
Printed in China by Toppan Leefung Printing Ltd., Dongguan City, Guangdong Province